RISKING THE DETECTIVE

THE BLUESTOCKING SCANDALS BOOK 6

ELLIE ST. CLAIR

♥ Copyright 2021 Ellie St Clair

All rights reserved.

This book or parts thereof may not be reproduced in any form, stored in any retrieval system, or transmitted in any form by any means—electronic, mechanical, photocopy, recording, or otherwise—without prior written permission of the publisher.

Facebook: Ellie St. Clair

Cover by AJF Designs

Do you love historical romance? Receive access to a free ebook, as well as exclusive content such as giveaways, contests, freebies and advance notice of pre-orders through my mailing list!

Sign up here!

Also By Ellie St. Clair

The Bluestocking Scandals
Designs on a Duke
Inventing the Viscount
Discovering the Baron
The Valet Experiment
Writing the Rake
Risking the Detective
A Noble Excavation

The Victorian Highlanders
Callum's Vow
Finlay's Duty
Adam's Call
Roderick's Purpose
Peggy's Love

Blooming Brides
A Duke for Daisy
A Marquess for Marigold
An Earl for Iris
A Viscount for Violet

The Blooming Brides Box Set: Books 1-4

The Unconventional Ladies
Lady of Mystery
Lady of Fortune
Lady of Providence
Lady of Charade

Happily Ever After
The Duke She Wished For
Someday Her Duke Will Come
Once Upon a Duke's Dream
He's a Duke, But I Love Him
Loved by the Viscount
Because the Earl Loved Me

Happily Ever After Box Set Books 1-3
Happily Ever After Box Set Books 4-6

Searching Hearts
Duke of Christmas (prequel)
Quest of Honor
Clue of Affection
Hearts of Trust
Hope of Romance
Promise of Redemption

Searching Hearts Box Set (Books 1-5)

Standalone
Unmasking a Duke
The Stormswept Stowaway
Christmastide with His Countess
Her Christmas Wish
Merry Misrule

House of Devon
A Touch of Temptation

CHAPTER 1

LONDON, 1824

"Take a seat, Miss Castleton."

Madeline straightened her spine to sit as tall as she could.

She would not be cowed. Not today. Not anymore.

She summoned all of her strength and courage. "As this is my office, Mr. Drake, I would invite *you* to sit."

He raised his eyebrows, and she got the impression that he was passing some judgment upon her, although he didn't say anything that would belie what was lurking beyond those dark, expressionless eyes.

The silent battle of wills did not last long, for it seemed Mr. Drake soon realized he would gain nothing from it.

It was a new state of affairs for Madeline. A small step, but one that was immeasurably important.

He sat. As did she, across from him, behind the desk that formed a barrier between them, one that she currently appreciated more than she wanted to admit.

"Now, then," he said, folding his hands in his lap over the notebook that sat upon those impossibly hard, rigid thighs she was doing her very best to ignore, "tell me, where were you last night between two o'clock and five o'clock in the morning?"

Madeline's chin shot up at the question. "Pardon me?"

He didn't react — no sigh, no deep breath, no sign of annoyance whatsoever. He simply repeated himself.

Madeline narrowed her eyes, refusing to answer his question until she understood why he was asking it. "Mr. Drake, why are you here?"

"To investigate the vandalism that occurred in your factory, Miss Castleton. That was why you requested my presence."

He might not have shown any emotion, but Madeline couldn't help her irritation at his explanation, as though she was not intelligent enough to understand the situation.

"Clearly," she said dryly. "However, I ask, Mr. Drake—"

"Drake. Just Drake."

"Drake, then. I ask, because I am unsure as to why my whereabouts would be important."

"The whereabouts of everyone involved in this case are important."

"Mr. Dra— that is, Drake, *I* am the vic—"

No. She would never again use that word to describe herself.

"I asked you here."

"There have been many times that we detectives have been summoned by the very person who perpetrated the crime."

Madeline rubbed the crease between her eyes, unable to keep her expression as void as that of the detective in front of her.

"Alice said you could help," she tried again.

"I can."

"Then why—"

"Miss Castleton," he said, leaning forward, his dark eyes probing into her. "It is my turn to ask you — what do you want from me here?"

"To determine who is trying to destroy my business, quite obviously."

"Your father's business."

She sighed quietly, not wanting him to detect her impatience. "It is my father's business, yes, but he has entrusted it to me while he is away at Bath."

"With the mother of your friend, the very Mrs. Luxington with whom both are acquainted."

She shot him a look as a streak of surprise sliced through her. "Do you know everything?"

"I try to make it my business to," he replied, the slightest hint of smugness tightening his lips. It was the first bit of emotion she had seen from him throughout this encounter.

"Well. No matter who he is with," she said, drawing herself up and forcing what she hoped was some confidence to her face, "he always intended that I take over the business, anyway. This seemed to be a good time for a trial."

"Ah," he said, a dawning raining over his features, which were far too dark and mysterious for his own good, "that is why this is of such great importance to you. Because it could cause your father to lose confidence in your ability to look after Castleton Stone."

"Mr. Drake," she began, taking a breath. If she was going to be the head of this business, she must begin acting like she was.

"Drake."

"*Drake*," she repeated, her frustration now clear. Why did he have to be so contrary? "Why I called you here does not matter. What matters is that I *did* call you here, and that it is your job to determine what has occurred. I can assure you that there is no reason whatsoever for me to have played any part in this. So, could we please move on to finding the true culprit?"

"That is all well and good, Miss Castleton, but in order for me to solve this crime, I must be able to determine whether anything of importance occurred at the time of the issue. Now, would you like me to do my *job*, as you say?"

"Of course," she said quietly, bowing her head, feeling foolish that she had challenged him so.

He sat back in his chair and tilted his head to the side, leaning his temple upon his index finger as he studied her. "You did not ask me here to pity you, did you?"

"*Pity* me?" she said, her exclamation harsher than she had intended.

She didn't have to ask just why he would pity her. She already knew. He knew. Everyone knew.

"Yes. The rest of London does, do they not?"

She dipped her head. Her stupidity, her naivety would follow her around for the rest of her life. This detective's opinion shouldn't matter, and yet she couldn't help the shame that washed over her at the awareness of what he likely thought of her.

He was intelligent enough to solve crimes that perplexed most, while she hadn't even been able to figure out that the man who had claimed to be Lord Donning had actually swindled her into marriage only to steal her dowry, before attempting to fatally poison her in order to inherit all of her wealth.

"It was not your fault, Miss Castleton," Drake said now, his voice surprisingly gentle, causing her to snap her head back up to look at him. "You were not the first woman to be deceived by Kurt Maxfeld — known to you as Lord Stephen Donning — but, fortunately, you will be the last."

"Thanks to Alice and her husband," Madeline murmured, before conceding, "and you."

"You showed great bravery as well," Drake said, but Madeline couldn't meet his gaze.

She knew he was just doing his job, playing the sympathetic detective. She had done nothing that denoted any bravery whatsoever. She had fled. She had hidden. Meanwhile, her friend had caught the man who had ruined Madeline's life.

"We are not here to discuss Lord Donning — or Kurt Maxfeld or whatever his name is," Madeline said, not able to bear the topic any longer. "We are here to discuss my business."

"Your father's business," he corrected her once more, and Madeline had to take a deep breath to keep herself from telling him exactly what she thought of his barbed comments.

"Very well, Miss Castleton," he said, his knee bouncing ever so slightly as he crossed an ankle over the other one, "will you tell me, then, where you were last night between two and five in the morning?"

She closed her eyes for but a moment to regain her focus.

"I was at home," she said, providing the truth. "Reading."

Finally, it seemed that she had captured his attention. "Reading, you say? You were not sleeping?"

"I was not," she said, shaking her head. "I find it difficult to sleep after... last year."

"When you were nearly poisoned to death," he said, not seeming to understand the implication that she would prefer not to speak of it. "I suppose that would cause someone to be afraid to go to sleep."

"I am not afraid," she said softly. "I just... I dream when I sleep. Nightmares, I suppose you can say. It is much easier to stay awake."

"If only it were possible to live without sleep," he said, and she couldn't tell whether or not he was making fun of her. "Was anyone in the house with you?"

"I have an aunt who lives with us," she explained. "My father's older sister. She never married and came to us when my mother passed. She was home but was in bed by nine o'clock. I did not see her nor speak to her until morning. We also have a live-in maid who…" her cheeks warmed slightly as she was about to say that the maid helped her undress, "who helped me prepare for the night to come before she retired herself."

"I see," he murmured, his eyebrows rising ever so slightly at the discussion of her nightly activities. "Very good, then. You were nowhere near Castleton Stone?"

"Not after five o'clock in the evening. Why are you continuing to question me about this?" she couldn't help but ask.

"We've discussed this. That is my job."

"I am not a suspect, Mr. Drake. This is my business."

"I never said you were a suspect."

"Then why are you treating me as one?"

He leaned forward in the chair, and she wished that he didn't unnerve her. He was taller than she, his shoulders broad, but he was not an overly large man. There was just something about him… something that she couldn't quite describe but that was so mysterious, so intimidating, that it took everything within her to keep from shrinking back away from him and his dark, piercing stare that seemed to only ask questions without providing any answers in return.

"I just find it interesting, Miss Castleton, that the moment you take more control of this business, it is put into jeopardy."

She dropped her gaze. "I would assume that my father's rivals are taking advantage of his absence."

"And the fact that he left a woman in charge."

Madeline eyed him again. "Are you condemning him for doing so?"

He sat back again, assessing her as though her response held much interest for him. "It is not for me to judge, Miss Castleton. Simply observe. And my observations tell me that most men would see a woman at the helm of a business to have weakened it."

Madeline nodded. "I am aware of the fact."

Drake opened his mouth, likely about to ask Madeline another question about motive this time perhaps, but was prevented from continuing by a new presence.

"I say, that is quite enough."

They both turned in unison to find her cousin standing at the doorway. His familiar presence sent a wave of relief washing over her. She had hoped he would be here for this particular interview. He was nothing but loyal.

"And you are…"

Drake was clearly not impressed, perhaps because he could no longer continue his bullying with another man, part of her family, in the room.

"Bennett Castleton," he said, his disdain for Drake apparent as his pinched nose somehow elongated as he stared down at the detective. "Miss Castleton's cousin. It appears, sir, that you have upset her and I would ask you to leave."

Sensing the tension that immediately filled the air of the office, Madeline stood and crossed over to her cousin, placing a hand on his arm. "It's all right, Bennett," she said quietly. "I called him here."

"You did?" he said, his voice registering shock as he stared at her, mouth agape. "But why?"

"Because half of the product within our factory was *vandalized*," she said, wishing they were not having this argument, as slight as it was, in front of Drake. "We need to determine who did it and why, so that we can regain control of the business."

"And you think *he* can help us?" Bennett asked, tilting his head over toward Drake.

Madeline took a breath, suddenly wondering if Bennett's presence was helpful after all. "I hope he can. He is a Bow Street constable."

"A runner?" Bennett questioned in surprise.

"We are not fond of the term," Drake responded from where he still sat, no hint of malice in his voice.

"Very well, then," Bennett said with a deep breath. "Find out who did this to our stone. But please do not cause my cousin to feel any further guilt for what happened. She has been working tirelessly since my Uncle Ezra left for Bath."

"Why would she feel guilt, Mr. Castleton?" Drake asked, and Madeline had to restrain herself from rolling her eyes.

"I shall be fine, Bennett," she said softly. "We do not have much more to speak about." She looked over at Drake, who was watching her in turn. "At least not today."

Bennett looked back and forth between the two of them until finally, apparently satisfied, he pulled up a chair from the wooden table and sat down upon it next to the wall.

Drake eyed him until Bennett held up a hand.

"I shall say nothing. I am here to observe, and to offer my support when necessary."

"What type of support might you require, Miss Castleton?"

"I—"

Madeline was about to respond that she didn't actually need any, but Bennett interrupted once more.

"Well, now, Drake, you are aware of all that happened to Madeline earlier this year, are you not?"

Madeline could only hope that her look toward him

conveyed her wish that he not speak of it any longer. She and Drake had only just gotten past the topic of conversation.

Now Drake turned and stared at Madeline instead. "Do you require assistance in regard to the actions of Maxfeld?"

"No," she said, unable to help the rush of gratitude at being addressed directly. "I shall be fine."

"Now, Madeline," Bennett began, but Drake quickly moved on, ignoring her cousin.

"Miss Castleton, if you are so convinced that Castleton Stone's rivals are at fault, why do you not tell me of them?" he asked, and Madeline sighed, relieved at the turn of the conversation to something that was not only focused on her, but could actually lead to a determination of the culprit.

"There is another stone company that has been a rival to ours for a number of years — Treacle Stone," she explained. "At the helm is a man named Jeremiah Treacle. He has recently inherited the business from his father. While Mr. Treacle, the elder, and my father have always had a great deal of respect for one another, Mr. Jeremiah Treacle does not seem to have any qualms in putting the success of his business over any relationship. I would suggest starting there."

"Absolutely," Bennett said, nodding his head in the corner. "Treacle. It has to be. Why, I would—"

"Thank you, Miss Castleton, Mr. Castleton," Drake said, straightening his serviceable black coat as he rose. Madeline's fingers strangely itched to reach out and feel the gold buttons to see if they were as smooth as they looked to be from where she sat. As Drake stepped away from the chair, a finger of sunlight bounced in through the window and glanced off them, causing her to squint.

"When will you go?" she asked, straightening her dress as she stood.

"When I am able to," he said cryptically, and she had the

feeling that he was dismissing her. "Good day, Miss Castleton."

She knew, then, that this act of vandalism in her factory meant nothing to him, and that if he did follow up, it would not be with any true level of importance.

"May I accompany you when you do?" she forced herself to call after him, and he stopped, turned around, and shook his head with a benevolent smile.

"I will come, as well!" Bennett added, holding a finger in the air.

"I am the detective here, Miss Castleton," Drake said, turning around and looking at her from over his shoulder. "You are a stone manufacturer. I will focus on my job. You should focus on yours."

And with that dismissal, he was out the door, leaving her with her fists at her side, her lips tight together, and shame in her heart.

CHAPTER 2

*D*rake couldn't help the muttered curse that sprang from his lips as he stepped out of the wooden building with its red thatched roof that was Castleton Stone.

He did take a moment to admire the assembly of statues out in the yard — a Greek god of some kind reclining on his stone throne, beard flowing in front of him with water pouring out of an urn in his hand; a family crest; and a giant floral motif that seemed to be a fountain of some sort. In front of it all a head of a likely important man sat on a pedestal, high above them all.

They were statues of the finest order and were, as the company boasted, nearly imperceptible from true, original stone.

He wondered what would happen if Ezra Castleton did, in fact, leave his daughter in charge permanently. This was obviously a test, and one that Drake was not sure Miss Castleton was going to pass.

Drake had known of Miss Castleton's story before he had actually met the woman. She had married after a quick courtship to a man who had been accepted as the long-lost Earl of Donning.

A man who had proven himself to be an imposter, since he already had a wife at home in a small village not far outside of London. His marriage to Miss Castleton was null and void, and she was now ruined in the eyes of all those who knew her name — which all of London did, now that the scandal had been spread through the tabloids. Drake wondered if the intrigue had helped the business or worsened it. He supposed the father must have some degree of faith in the woman, if he had left her in charge.

At the very least, the short union hadn't seemed to have left Miss Castleton in the family way, which she must have been grateful for. She had been damaged, but it could have been worse.

Not that any of it had any bearing on his job.

Except... he knew it was the protector within him, one of the very reasons he worked for Bow Street, but after meeting with her face-to-face, he couldn't resist the urge to try to help her, to keep anyone from hurting her further. The woman had been through far more than she deserved, that much was true, and through no fault of her own.

Drake couldn't help but feel, however, that somehow she had allowed herself to be taken advantage of. He thought of Alice Luxington, and the way she had taken charge of her life and fought for her love and her livelihood. He thought of his own life, and what drove him to find justice wherever he could. He thought of all of the people who came to him for help for crimes that had been committed against them.

If Madeline Castleton truly wished to run her father's business and he, in turn, was leaving it to her, then she had the ability. But did she have the determination? Of that, Drake wasn't sure. She had been quick to leave it all to marry the man she thought had been Lord Donning. What had changed that would convince her that this was the correct course for her life?

He sighed, running a hand through his hair before replacing his cap upon it.

It wasn't for him to be concerned with. All that should matter to him was the case itself.

A case that was barely a case. So someone had knocked over a few statues. It happened every day, all over London. He didn't see why he should be concerned about it as a detective. He would ask a few questions to appease the woman, he decided. He would ensure that she was looked after, that she wouldn't come into danger again.

Then he would move on to other cases. To major thefts, murders, assaults. A little vandalized stone was hardly worth noting.

And not worth exacting justice for.

No, justice was best found for those who hurt others to such an extent that it could not be qualified. Those injustices were what drove him.

Those injustices were worth fighting for.

And he had promised he would never stop doing so.

"I AM A FOOL."

"You are not a fool. You are one of the most intelligent women I know, if not *the* most intelligent woman I know. So please stop saying that."

Madeline sighed and took a seat on the plush sofa in her friend Alice's parlor, sinking back into the sumptuous pillows that were apparently made for feeling sorry for oneself. It was Alice's favorite room of the house she shared with her husband, Mr. Benjamin Luxington, and often where they found themselves when Madeline came to call.

"How was your meeting with Mr. Drake?"

"Drake — no Mister," Madeline said, lifting a brow as she recalled the way he had told her to address him.

"Oh yes, that's right," Alice said, tilting her dark head to the side as she leaned forward on her writing stool toward Madeline, her chin on top of her fist. "I always forget. I wonder why. He must have a truly terrible first name."

"I can't say I care whatsoever," Madeline said, although that was something of a lie. "Do you see him often?" she asked, attempting nonchalance. She knew she should have no interest in the detective other than on a professional level, but there was something altogether... intriguing about him. It was as though the lack of emotion displayed upon the surface tempted her into seeking to discover what was lurking below it.

"Not really," Alice said, shaking her head. "He was at our wedding of course — well, *both* of our weddings, and we attempted to ask him to dinner a time or two, but he was always busy. From what I can tell, the man doesn't do anything but work."

"As a detective."

"Right," Alice said, nodding. "So, did he help you?"

"Not really — not yet," Madeline said, shaking her head. "In fact, I received the impression that he thought I was wasting his time and that *I* had something to do with the vandalism. It was as though he was interrogating *me*."

"Interrogating you?" Alice lifted her eyebrows, her warm brown eyes piercing into Madeline. "Why would you say that?"

"The questions he was asking me — where I was, why the company was suddenly having troubles now that I'm in charge, that sort of thing," Madeline said with a sigh. "And then there was the manner in which he said it. There was no hint of warmth nor any compassion present."

Except for the moment in which he told her that Stephen — no, Kurt Maxfeld, his true name — had been at fault for the past. Drake had shown a moment of softness then, before it had quickly vanished.

But that was not a subject she currently felt like discussing.

"Truly, though, who do you think would do such a thing to you? To go to the point of ruining work you had completed?" Alice asked, fixing her stare on Madeline.

"Perhaps Jeremiah Treacle," Madeline said with a shrug. "I'm not sure who else at this point." She caught her lip between her teeth when it threatened to tremble anew. "But *why*, Alice? Why does all of this keep happening to me? What am I doing wrong with my life?"

Alice stood and crossed over to Madeline, bending in front of her and placing her hands on her knees.

"Nothing at all, Madeline," she said, holding a finger up toward her before she could say anything else. "And as for the business, your father would never have left it in your hands if he did not have confidence in you to succeed. He has spent years building Castleton, and he would only leave his baby in the hands he trusted the most."

Madeline nodded, wishing she could believe Alice's words, but despite her friend's well-meaning intentions, they only served to further worry her. For Alice was right. Her father had spent his life building the stone business. What if Madeline destroyed it in just a few weeks?

"You'll figure this out," Alice said confidently. "And did you not tell me that you had a new idea you wanted to try?"

"Well..." Madeline hedged, "I do. It's a new product. The current Castleton Stone is not very malleable and we must press it into molds to be fired in the kilns. I think with a few changes, we could create material that could actually be sculpted by hand before firing, to allow for greater originality. Not for all pieces, but for some it would be like owning a piece of art instead of a piece of architecture. But perhaps now is not the time. Not with my father away and with the vandalism that occurred—"

"What better time would there be?" Alice asked, and Madeline had to smile at her friend, who only saw opportunities in risks, and not the potential downfalls. She wished she could be as spontaneous and carefree, but she just didn't have it within her. "Take your idea to your factory and see what you can do. This new stone — tell me, are you thinking of doing more sculpting yourself?"

"I think I would," Madeline said slowly, trying not to display the excitement that was already beginning to simmer in her belly. Sometimes — when she needed a respite from the numbers and precision that formed most of her day — she took the time to visit the workshop of the business, to sit among the artists and sculpt her own creations. It wasn't out of Castleton stone, but rather the clay that they used to create molds. She didn't know what they did with all of her work. Some her father had lined on the bookshelves around his office; others she took home, and the remaining were likely sold to those who couldn't afford anything worthwhile.

She didn't really care one way or another. She sculpted because it gave her a sense of peace to do the work, peace that she never found anywhere else. "It will all be a test. We have tried some formulas with it before, but I think with this one addition…"

She began to ponder it anew, her heart quickening with the thought that she could create something that would impress her father, and make him realize with all certainty that she had the wherewithal to manage Castleton Stone. Could she go ahead with this? What would he think?

More importantly, what would everyone else think?

Unfortunately, she was well aware of what her name was currently associated with. Ridicule. Scorn. Naivety.

She had been so caught up with a man who had given her just a little bit of attention that she hadn't seen beyond what he had showcased to her, and in the process, she had nearly lost her life.

If Alice and Benjamin had not found her when they did...

"Madeline?"

Madeline blinked as she re-focused on her friend.

"Where did you go?" Alice asked with a slight laugh, her dimples indenting as she eyed her knowingly — except, she didn't know. No one could realize the dark places to which Madeline's mind wandered sometimes.

And it was not something she had any care to share. The thoughts were crippling enough without being released in the open.

"Nowhere," Madeline said, forcing a smile. "I'm right here."

"Did your thoughts have anything to do with a handsome detective?" Alice asked, winging up an eyebrow.

"A handsome detective? You mean Drake?"

"Of course I mean Drake!" Alice said, her eyes twinkling mischievously as she twirled around on her writing stool. "He has all of the qualities for a perfect hero — he is dark, mysterious, oh-so-serious... were you not intrigued?"

"Well of course I was intrigued," Madeline admitted. "Who wouldn't be by a man who shows no emotion, who doesn't seem bothered by anything or anyone? And what type of man becomes a Bow Street Runner? How does one even get into such a profession? And why? Furthermore—"

She stopped when Alice threw back her head in a loud, jolly laugh.

"What?"

"When I asked if you were intrigued, I didn't realize you were already smitten with the man!"

"Smitten!" Madeline exclaimed, outrage in her tone. "I am far from smitten. In fact, I was actually rather annoyed that he barely took me seriously. If I did not actually need the help, I would be of a mind to tell him to leave it be if it was so far beneath him."

"Oh, Madeline," Alice said, her smile falling. "I never meant—"

"It's fine," Madeline said, shaking her head, reining in her emotion when she realized just how juvenile her outburst must have sounded. "I am just irritated, is all. I'm sure this vandalism is nothing, just some mischief-makers who managed to make their way into our factory and behead some statues. I have a man on guard at night now, watching over things."

"Well, that should be helpful," Alice said. "If there is anything I can do—"

"I know," Madeline said with a warm smile, feeling guilty that she had become cross at her friend, who was just trying to help. "Thank you."

"Good afternoon, ladies."

Both women looked up to find Alice's husband, Benjamin, standing in the doorway. He greeted Madeline briefly, but he only had eyes for one woman — Alice. He crossed over to her, leaning down to kiss her quickly on the lips, and Madeline inwardly sighed. Oh, to have a man look at her as Benjamin did Alice. This, she realized now, was true love.

If only she had known such a thing a year ago, when Lord Donning had begun courting her. She had been swept off her feet by his quick, intense courtship. Madeline knew she had often been described as a delicate beauty, but she was aware that the reserve that kept her from sharing too much with others often scared off potential suitors. There was also the fact that while her father possessed a great fortune and had always paid for the very best education — where she had met Alice — he was still a merchant, albeit a merchant who felt that his daughter was worth far more than anyone within their own social class.

So when an earl — an earl! — had been interested in his daughter, he had been just as quick as Madeline to entertain the idea of their marriage.

Until all fell to disaster.

But never again, she vowed.

For she was clearly not one who could be trusted with her emotions. She had thought she had found true love, when it had been anything but.

Her intelligence, her intuition, her inference — had all failed her.

Now, she had to just do all she could to pick up the pieces and put together a life that would be worth living — even without the love she had always longed for.

Thank goodness she had the business.

Now she just had to hold onto it before it was as ruined as the rest of her life.

CHAPTER 3

Drake tested the railing as he climbed the stairs on the rickety front porch.

A board creaked beneath his weight, and he made a note on his ever-lengthening list of things to fix when he had some time.

He hadn't been here nearly as much as he should be, for which he chastised himself. He was working tirelessly to try to right all of London's wrongs — the very least he could do was to take proper care of the people who depended upon him, the people who had been there for him when he could have been left alone in the world.

Before he had a chance to ruminate any further however, the door swung open.

"Drake, luv, how are you?" His aunt surprised him as she enveloped him in an embrace as he stepped through the door. She was the only one he would ever allow so close. He had developed love for his aunt and uncle before he had learned how to turn it off, and therefore, these were the two people who were allowed within the thick, high, sturdy walls he had built around himself.

"I am fine, as always, Aunt Mabel," he said, kissing the top of her head. "Uncle Andrew." He nodded at the man, who returned the gesture.

"Come in, come in," his aunt said, leading him into the room, and he took a seat on the threadbare sofa as he gazed up at the two images that stared back at him from over the fireplace.

One was of himself. It had been sketched at a carnival or something of the sort, not created for anything worth keeping, but it had been all they had ever been able to commission.

And so it stayed, in its place of honor, surrounded by a frame his uncle had fashioned himself.

Next to it was a painting of his parents. It was crude, not displaying them in their full likeness, but was enough to remind Drake of them... and of his purpose. A purpose from which he could not stray.

To right the wrongs.

To fight for justice.

To protect the innocent.

"Tell us, what has kept you busy, lately?" his aunt said as she bustled into the room carrying a tea tray. As she bent, Drake caught sight of her hands, the veins within the wrinkles appearing to him suddenly, as though somehow he had missed the fact that his aunt and uncle were aging, that they should be better cared for – by him.

"Work, as usual," he said, taking the offered cup and sipping it, the warm liquid, spice with cinnamon and clove, a heartfelt grounding, surging together the past and the present in one cup of home. "And you?"

"The same," his aunt said, drawing a blanket over her lap as his uncle took a seat in the chair across from them. His teacup looked like a doll's in his large-knuckled hands which had spent their life working, building, placing one stone upon another. He was a builder, a laborer, creating something out of nothing, fixing wrongs in his own way.

"Uncle Andrew," Drake said, a thought suddenly occurring to him, "what do you think of the fabricated stone that has made an appearance over the past few years? Does it hold up, or is it all a ploy?"

His uncle lifted one bushy brow. "What's the sudden interest?" he asked, and Drake held his stare. His uncle had been greatly disappointed when Drake hadn't followed in his footsteps, learning the trade from him, but Drake had other priorities — priorities which did not involve building.

"It has to do with a case."

"I see." His uncle's gaze became shuttered again, and he looked out through the window as though contemplating his answer. "Depends on the company," he said, looking back at Drake now. "Some are of high quality and more durable than any stone to be found from the land. Others do nothing but steal a man's hard-earned riches. If it's cheap enough for most to afford, then it will not last, son. Nothing that is cheap or easy will stand the test of time, let me tell you."

Drake nodded, hoping to stop his uncle before he began reciting his views on life — views that he felt everyone should follow, most especially Drake himself.

"You are right, Uncle, absolutely," he said with a nod, hoping that quick agreement would spare him. It was not that he didn't appreciate his uncle sharing his wisdom with him — it was that he had already heard it countless times before.

"I wish neither of you had to work," Drake said, rubbing the stubble on his jaw, stubble that he should have shaved but kept forgetting to.

"Oh, we like the work," his aunt said, although somehow, he doubted cleaning laundry for others could be considered enjoyable. "What would we do without it?"

"I'm not sure," he said, raising an eyebrow. "Sit? Enjoy life?"

His aunt laughed at that, while his uncle simply snorted, and Drake supposed that they had a point. They knew nothing but work, so how were they to learn any differently?

"Now, tell us, any young women in your life these days?" his aunt asked, her lips curled up expectantly, and the word 'no' was on Drake's lips, but suddenly, an image appeared in his mind, one unbidden and not at all welcomed — Madeline Castleton.

He shook his head to clear it. She was simply in his thoughts because he had just met with her. For she was *not* a woman he would ever consider romantically. He preferred strong women, women who were clear-minded, focused, determined.

Miss Castleton was a frail beauty if there ever was one. He had a feeling that her wispy, light-blond hair would almost disintegrate if he were to touch it, not that his hands would have any invitation to come close to her. She had the palest skin, as though it had never seen the sun, her frame lacking strength of any sort. Though her eyes, as blue as the sky on a clear day, were difficult to forget. They cut through a man when they focused upon him, as though they could see right through his suit of armor — even if it was, in his case, a black jacket over buff trousers.

"No," he finally said, shaking his head to his aunt's hopeful stare. "No one."

"Oh, Drake," she said, her smile falling. "I do wish you would take more care to find yourself a bride. You need a good woman in your life."

"That is why I have you," he said, attempting humor, but she batted his arm.

"You know what I mean. And I will not be here forever."

"Don't say that," he said, his tone more curt than he had intended, but he would far prefer not to speak of such things.

"Drake," she said, leaning toward him, "your parents would want you to be happy. You know that, yes?"

He nodded, not trusting himself to actually respond to her suggestion without any emotion.

"Besides," his uncle added, "how do you know that you are not going to find yourself in trouble? Your aunt and I worry every day that you will get on the wrong side of the wrong person, find yourself in the graveyard next to your parents. Do you know what they would say to us, if we allowed such a thing to happen at your age? Perhaps if you had a woman to come home to, a family… you would take more care."

"If such a thing happened, know that it would not be your fault," Drake said gruffly, ignoring the last suggestion, but his aunt and uncle stared at him with such sadness that he could no longer meet their eyes. "But onto more important things — what does a man have to do around here to get some dinner?"

* * *

DRAKE OPENED the door of his small house, both welcoming and abhorring the silence that awaited.

He didn't spend much time here, in the one-story house near Bow Street he had bought a year ago, when he had saved just enough for his own space. Most of his investigations took place not during the sunlit hours of the day, but in the dark of night, when the criminal element emerged. It was the time when the shadows provided cover for the most nefarious of deeds, but also when truths were revealed.

But not tonight. Tonight was quiet. So quiet that he even had time to ruminate on an act of vandalism that would normally be far too inconsequential for him to provide any time for.

Which worried him. Whenever London seemed quiet, it usually meant that something was in store, something brewing that threatened to cause more turmoil than he would have liked.

He threw the wad of money on the side table as he entered — money that he had attempted to give to his aunt and uncle, but they had refused, telling him that if he left it with them again, they would only give it away.

He had taken it, but would go around the next day and ensure that any debts they had owing would be paid. That much he could do for the two people who had taken him in when he had no one, when he had been left by himself. If it wasn't for them, he would have grown up in an orphanage, alone and forgotten.

He owed them everything.

It was the other reason why he worked as tirelessly as he did. If he was going to fight for justice, then he might as well get paid enough for it that he could help to support them.

Even if it meant submitting to the worries of a fragile blond beauty, her pesky protector of a cousin, and a factory full of fake stone.

CHAPTER 4

Dear Madeline,

I hope all is well in London with the factory. I am quite enjoying myself in Bath, I must tell you. It has been far too long — years too long — since I have taken any time away from the business. I am grateful to you, Daughter, for providing me with the ability to leave Castleton Stone in such good hands. I have faith that you cannot only keep the business running, but will make sure that it thrives.

Bennett promised to help in whatever you may need. He may not have the head or the heart for the stone business like you do, but as you know, he will do anything for this family, and I trust that he will be there to support you in every way.

I shall not be gone for too much longer — a few weeks at most.

Wishing you all my love,
Your Doting Father

Madeline closed her eyes and allowed her head to fall so far forward that it was resting against the desk, the paper sandwiched between the wood and her forehead.

Her father had such faith in her. She should appreciate it,

welcome it — and she did. Most women would never be afforded such responsibility.

But she was failing him. She knew that.

Even as she closed her eyes, she heard the knock on the door, the clerk once again calling her, telling her that another client was awaiting her.

"A Lord Bainbridge, Miss Castleton!"

She groaned. Another client, eager for his stone. Stone which had been destroyed.

They were working as hard as they could to catch up in the factory, to replace the broken sculptures and fulfill all of the orders. But it wasn't enough. Not without bringing in more hands, and even then, new bodies would require training, training that she just didn't have time for. Besides that, it took four days to fire the stone in the kiln, which could only fit so many pieces.

She took a deep breath and sat up, fixing her hair as best she could to welcome the visitor. "Please send him in, Clark!"

She straightened her spine and braced herself to explain all she could to the client, and hopefully stave him off for a few days, until they had time to shore up their supply, or at least come somewhat close to it.

Then she had a visit to make. She needed this mystery solved, and she needed it solved *now*.

It had been three days since she had seen Drake. Three days since she had told him of her problem. Three days since he had promised to look into it.

And in three days, she had not received one word in return from him.

So, she would just have to visit him instead.

* * *

DRAKE WAS ITCHING for a case to solve.

A good case. One that would take all of his attention, all of his deduction, so that his mind would be focused instead of free to wander to places it had no business wandering.

Or, should he say, to people he had no business focusing on.

Like Madeline Castleton.

He was only interested in helping her because she had been so wronged, he reasoned with himself. Yes, he had been able to ensure last year that her scandal had come to a satisfying conclusion, but once a reputation was so ruined, there was no putting it back together again. At least, not in this case. This was one wrong he could not right.

He had meant to follow up with her on her current situation, to speak with the rival, Treacle, that she was so sure was behind it all, but he had not yet found the time to do so.

Or so he told himself.

He also told himself that it all had nothing to do with the fact that he hadn't been able to stop thinking about her, that something about her — maybe it was that she was so slight and unimposing – threatened to slip through any crack that appeared in the wall around him.

For he was resolved that no one would ever do so.

"Something bothering you today, Drake?"

He looked up to find Marshall, the only other constable present in the Magistrate's Office on Bow Street today, looking at him thoughtfully from beneath his bushy red eyebrows.

"No," he said, shaking his head. "Why would you think that?"

Marshall lifted a shoulder. "You've got a frown on your face the likes of which I've never seen before."

"Just bored," he said with a sigh. "Waiting for something big to come in."

"Well," Marshall said, drawing out the word, looking

beyond Drake's shoulder. "Seems to me that something has come in, although *big* wouldn't be the word for it."

Drake hadn't even heard the door open, and yet before he turned to see who the new arrival was, somehow he knew, without looking, that she would be standing there.

"Hello." Her voice, soft and whispery, floated across the room to him, tickling his ears and causing the hair on the back of his neck to stand on end. "I am here to see Drake."

Marshall, who was facing her, rose from his desk and approached. "Well, hello, my lady," he said, bowing before her. "How are you today?"

"She's not a lady," Drake called out, imagining Miss Castleton's reaction.

"Pardon me?" she said, lifting an eyebrow as he stood and began to walk toward her.

"I said you're not a lady," Drake repeated matter-of-factly. "You are the daughter of a merchant. Therefore, not a lady."

Miss Castleton tilted her head to the side while looking up at him. "You are correct in that, of course," she said, "however, there is one statement that I would disagree with."

"Oh?"

"I am a merchant's daughter, yes," she said, lifting her chin, "but I would also qualify that by saying I am a merchant myself."

Drake couldn't help it. His lips quirked up at the corners, stretching themselves into quite a foreign expression.

"Why, Drake, I do believe you are smiling!" Marshall said, awe in his voice before turning to Miss Castleton with interest. "I say, my dear, who *are* you?"

"Madeline Castleton, of Castleton Stone."

"Oh, yes, I have heard of you," Marshall said, leaning in toward her. "Quite a good quality product you fashion, I hear. Takes some time to fabricate, though, does it not?"

"Some time, yes," she said in her gentle, quiet voice,

"although not nearly as long as the evolution of natural stone, now does it?"

At that, Marshall threw back his head and laughed, while Miss Castleton smiled knowingly at him.

"Nicholas Marshall," he said, bowing to her once again, even though they had all established that it was not necessary.

"Well, Mr. Marshall," she said with a nod of her head, "are you a constable as well?"

"I am."

"Perhaps you would be interested in a case, then," she said, avoiding looking over at Drake, "since it seems that there are no other detectives here who have any desire to help me."

There was a spark in her eyes and a set to her jaw, and Drake knew, then, how much courage it had likely taken for her to come seek him out again, and he was immediately regretful that he hadn't done more for her.

"My apologies, Miss Castleton," he said, linking his fingers together behind his back. "I have not been as attentive to this case as I should have been."

She finally turned toward him, her blue eyes piercing into him.

"I understand, Drake, that an act of vandalism may not seem to be of great importance to you. However, it means everything to me, and to my business, and I require assistance. I may not have been clear the last time we spoke that I am willing to pay handsomely for such help."

"How handsomely?" Marshall cut in, leaning forward between them.

"Fifty pounds for your time, and another fifty if you actually catch the culprit," she said.

Drake could only blink.

It was too much — far too much for a case like this, or for a case at all.

He opened his mouth to tell her so, that he could never accept it — that *they* could never accept it — but then he was taken back to the week prior, to the visit to his aunt and uncle's. He was reminded of the creaky front steps, of the worn sofa, of the gnarled hands both of them lived with while they continued working when they should be taking this time to enjoy their lives. He could use that money. *They* could use that money.

There was no room for his pride. Before he could say anything, however, Marshall intervened.

"Well, then, Miss Castleton, I would be more than happy to find your culprit," Marshall said, reaching out a hand to shake hers. "Although I would have anyway, of course."

"Unfortunately, Marshall, the case has already been claimed," Drake said, reaching out and breaking their hands, fighting away the strange urge to prevent another man — even a man like Marshall, a friend and good-natured soul — from touching her. "Forgive me, Miss Castleton. Give me a second chance."

He attempted to smile at her, although he was aware that his smiles, especially those that were forced, often had the look of a cringe instead.

She eyed him for a moment of indecision before she finally nodded her head curtly.

"Very well," she said. "As you already know the particulars of the case, Drake, I would be pleased for your help — if you promise to remain committed."

"Of course," he murmured. "Why don't you come sit down?"

He held his hand out in front of him, gesturing toward the spare chair next to the corner table. She nodded and followed as Marshall began to amble back across the room to his own seat, releasing a low chuckle as he went.

"I would be correct in assuming, then, that you have made no progress?" she said, holding onto her reticule with both hands as she stared at him from across the table, and for a moment he felt like a chastised child, although he would ensure she had no idea that he felt any guilt.

"Not quite yet," he said, fidgeting with his quill pen. "Soon, I hope." He looked around her for a moment, wondering just how she had come to be here. "Are you alone, Miss Castleton?"

"I am."

"That helpful cousin of yours did not accompany you?"

"He did not," she said smartly. "Bennett is ever so helpful, but he is also…"

"Annoyingly overbearing?" Drake supplied with a lifted brow, and she laughed.

Her laugh was more of a trill, one that surprised him, shocking him with the way it sent corresponding tremors down his spine to the very base of it. It stopped far too quickly, however, as she slapped a hand over her mouth.

"Oh dear," she said, moving her hand to the side as she caught his gaze with hers. "I really shouldn't poke fun."

"You didn't poke fun," Drake observed. "I did. You simply laughed."

She sighed. "Even so. For all of his good qualities, I know that Bennett does not wholeheartedly approve of Father leaving me, a woman, in charge, and he believes that he must be ever-present in order to prevent me from doing anything foolhardy. I often become quite tired of it."

"Understandable. I also would not want someone continually looking over my shoulder to determine how I am doing my job."

He turned his head ever-so-slightly to catch Marshall

nearly leaning over his own desk in an attempt to listen in to their conversation. When he heard Drake's words, he turned back to his paperwork so quickly that the two front legs of the chair came crashing to the ground and he almost tumbled off it.

Unlike Marshall, however, Drake was able to keep hold of his curiosity, the only hint of his mirth the curl of one side of his lips.

"Miss Castleton, you should not be here, in this neighborhood, alone."

Her eyes widened. "This is the Bow Street Magistrate's Office — I can hardly think of a safer place in all of London!"

"In that, you are right, of course," he relented. "However, it is the getting here that I am more concerned about."

"I have men with me who will always ensure my safety," she said. "It is none of your concern."

"On the contrary, Miss Castleton. You have just hired me to do exactly this — keep you safe."

If it was possible, she rose up even taller.

"Let me be clear then, Drake. I have hired you not to look after me, but to determine who is doing my business harm. My hope is that you are able to catch the culprit and to inform me as to who it is. I also hope that you will be able to do so expediently, before my father returns and as our factory continues to bolster our inventory. Understood?"

He did not enjoy being ordered about by the woman, but he swallowed the simmering ball of ire.

"Understood, Miss Castleton."

"Very good. Before I leave, then, perhaps we should make a plan to visit Jeremiah Treacle."

"I already said, Miss Castleton, I will—"

But then he caught the look on her face — the one that held an arched eyebrow, her gaze down her nose as she regarded him as she likely would an errant supplier.

"Very well," he grumbled. "Tomorrow?"

"Tomorrow," she said with a firm nod. "I will meet you at Treacle Stone."

"No. We'll meet at the Castleton factory and we will go together," he said, just as firmly.

For a moment, they sat there, their eyes locked in a silent battle of wills once more, until finally, he relented. She was, after all, the client here.

"Very well," he sighed. "I will meet you there."

She rose and glided to the door, her skirts swaying behind her.

It took everything within Drake not to watch her leave.

As it happened, however, she had just reached the door when it opened for her, and the messenger called out, "A package for Drake!" which, mercifully, captured the whole of his attention.

"I'm Drake," he answered, passing the man a shilling as he took the box, carrying it back to his desk, forgetting, for a moment, about Miss Castleton and her surprising, silent strength.

"What is it?" Marshall called out, but Drake couldn't answer.

He was too busy staring at what the box before him contained.

CHAPTER 5

Madeline folded her white gloved hands in front of her as she took deep breaths while staring at the door of Treacle Stone.

She had been here only once since Jeremiah Treacle had taken over the business, but that had been with her father.

They had not been well received. She could hardly bear to imagine how Treacle would welcome her today, without her father accompanying her.

Madeline was aware that most men did not see a place for women in business.

But it was hard to consider how a man could be more vocal about such thoughts than Jeremiah Treacle.

She looked around busy Holburn Street for the detective. Her visit to Bow Street yesterday had been quite the revelation.

For she now realized just what motivated Drake. Money. She supposed it motivated everyone to some extent, although she was somewhat surprised. He had seemed the type who would be more encouraged by righting the wrongs of the world.

Which was why he had likely taken so long to come around. Her little problem would have seemed insignificant to him.

A thought suddenly occurred to her. What if he didn't show up today? What was she to do then? She rubbed at her temples as she decided she would simply have to take this on and face Jeremiah Treacle herself.

Although that was the last thing in the world she had any wish to do.

Conflict was not something Madeline Castleton relished.

To such an extent that it had nearly killed her.

But that was the past. This was now. Now she was going to run a business, and she was going to run it well.

"Miss Castleton?"

"Drake!" she exclaimed, whirling around to face him. "You startled me."

"You were in the midst of a daydream of some sort," he noted correctly, and heat filled her cheeks at her fanciful thoughts.

"I was ruminating, is all. Now, what is our plan?"

"Our plan?"

"Do not all detectives have a plan when they are questioning a subject?"

"I have a plan, yes, Miss Castleton. But that does not involve you. You can simply observe."

"I hardly think that will work!" she exclaimed, shocked that he would be so dense. He was supposed to be a brilliant man. "He knows who I am and will wonder why I am here, accompanying a detective. You do not mean to simply ask him straight out if he is at fault? That will never do, not at all."

"Do you have another suggestion?"

"I do, as a matter of fact," she said, pleased that he had asked, although she was well aware that he had done so sarcastically. "I was thinking that you could pretend to be a new partner of Castleton Stone. We can tell Treacle that we have a proposition for him."

"Oh, do we?" Drake said, although he couldn't completely hide his interest in her idea.

"We will tell him that we have a project we have been commissioned for, but that we do not currently have the capacity to complete it, and that we are suggesting a partnership. We can then see how he feels about our business, determine how successful his own is at the moment, and see if he knows anything at all about why we do not currently have the ability to take this on ourselves."

Madeline thought that flicker on Drake's face just might have been a hint of admiration.

"Not a bad plan," he muttered.

"So?" she asked, "can you do it?"

He grunted. "Of course I can do it. After you, Miss Castleton."

As they stepped into the building, Madeline couldn't help but compare the front lobby and the product within it to her own. From her recollections, Treacle Stone had always nearly — *nearly* — matched Castleton Stone in quality. But this selection of statues in the front gallery was subpar, the stone less than ordinary, chips here and there, the stone already failing. Jeremiah, it seemed, was cutting costs. Well, all the more clients for Castleton Stone, she decided.

She approached the clerk behind the desk, asking to see Mr. Treacle. When he asked who was there to visit, she simply said, "An admirer," and sensed Drake looking at her.

"You didn't think he would see you?"

"I couldn't be sure," she murmured. "He does not like dealing with women. Perhaps you should take the lead."

She didn't want to tell him that her heart was hammering against her chest, and while she was determined to be there, she didn't know how firm she could be in her resolve to wrest information from Treacle — particularly when she was well aware of the disdain that would be on his face as he regarded her.

Disdain she saw now as he stepped into the room.

"Miss Madeline Castleton," he said, a sneer that began on his lips and rolled off with his words, "or do you still prefer Lady Donning?"

His prominent teeth emerged then as he laughed long and loud, and Madeline went rigid, wishing a witty comeback would spring to her lips, but her normally full mind went blank.

"Let's go," Drake said, nodding his head to the door as he looked at her, apparently ignoring Treacle. "It doesn't appear that he has any interest in our proposal. We shall find another who is not so crude."

"A proposal?" Treacle said, lifting a brow as dark as the oily black hair on his head. "Have you not had enough of those, Miss Castleton? I must say, I am shocked to hear that you are still involved in Castleton Stone. If there is one thing a person needs to properly run a business, that is intuition and good judgment, is it not? And you, quite clearly, lack what is required. Then again, you are a *woman*, so I suppose you could be forgiven. It is not your fault."

Madeline was a statue. A useless, stone statue, which did nothing but break when knocked over.

For he was right. She did lack judgment. She did lack intuition. The only thing he was wrong about was that it was because she was a woman. For many women possessed both traits in spades, with the additional components of bravery and backbone added in — just look at Alice, or Alice's sister-in-law, Lady Essex, and her friends.

"I will come back alone," Drake muttered in Madeline's

ear, too low for Treacle to hear. "You should not be subjected to this."

Madeline finally forced herself to move, even if it was just shaking her head. If she was going to prove herself, then she had to overcome the worst that could be thrown at her — and there had been far worse than Jeremiah Treacle.

"It's fine," she said, although her voice was hardly more than a whisper. "I can do this."

But she couldn't seem to think of anymore to say. How was she to deny the truth of his words? How was she to pretend to be something she wasn't? She had never been the kind of woman who could put on a façade, who could provide a front that the world would accept. When she was happy, those with her knew by her laugh, her smile, her carefree nature.

When she was upset, all knew as well.

Just look at last year — everyone had been aware that she was in trouble before she herself did.

Drake ran his eyes down her, from her likely furrowed brow to her hands, which were clasped so tightly together she knew the skin across her knuckles would be tight and strained beneath her gloves.

His assessment of her concluded, he seemed convinced of her readiness, and he nodded shortly at her before turning around.

"Treacle," he said, his words short and clipped, as though he didn't have time to pander to the man. "We are here to present a mutually beneficial idea to you. Should you not have the inclination to even hear our offer, then we will leave. I believe, however, that you would be a fool to miss this opportunity at the expense of making a few poorly worded jokes regarding Miss Castleton and the hardship that befell her."

Treacle's eyes narrowed at Drake's words, just as Madeline's heart bloomed.

It was stupid to be moved by Drake's defense of her — this was a man who lived to defend and protect others — and yet, the fact that he considered the *situation* to be at fault and not her meant all the difference in the world.

"Very well," Treacle finally said, as though he was doing them a favor. "I shall hear your proposal, and then, if I do not like it, you will be gone."

He turned and began walking down a corridor to the back of the building, and Madeline and Drake exchanged a look before following him.

"You do not have to be here," he murmured as they walked side-by-side, and Madeline couldn't help but be grateful that, at least, she was here with him and not alone.

"I want to be," she said firmly. "This is my business, and I will ensure that it survives."

He nodded but didn't respond as they followed Treacle into an office.

It suited him, Madeline thought, as she took a seat in one of the chairs he pointed to that was situated around a square table. The walls were white, shined to perfection, the navy brocade fabric of the furniture that surrounded the office noticeably new. While Treacle was obviously creating lesser quality products, he was wasting no money on his own grandeur.

Madeline sat with her hands tightly gripping her reticule, while Drake took a much more relaxed posture in the seat next to her, his one leg crossed over the other in what she realized was likely a calculated move, one that was designed to put his subjects at ease with the conversation. She didn't know why, but she was comforted by his presence, while also quite drawn by his proximity.

Madeline took a breath and attempted to, at the very

least, drop her shoulders from where they had heightened to her ears, so tense she was.

"Now," Treacle said, sitting across from them and interlacing his fingers as he placed his hands on the desk. He looked at Drake. "Who are you, and what are you doing here?"

"I am John Smith," Drake said, and Madeline's gaze shot to him incredulously. Really? Of all the names he could choose, he *would* be so boring.

Treacle's raised eyebrows showed that he obviously didn't believe him, but he waved his hand forward lazily for Drake to continue.

"I am a new partner of Miss Castleton's and it was my idea to see if you would like to be involved in this project. Castleton Stone recently won a commission for the stone to be used in the refurbishment of one of the palaces."

That had Treacle sitting up straighter.

"Oh? Which one?"

"I cannot say," Drake said cryptically. "But suffice it to say, it will be a most prestigious project."

"I have not heard of such a thing."

"That is because they did not tender out any of the work. It was all appointed."

Treacle looked from Drake to Madeline and then back at Drake.

"So why come to me for this? This should be a victory for you."

"It is," Madeline said dryly. "Believe me, Treacle, I would have preferred *not* to come."

"But, alas," Drake said with a sigh, the man who rarely showed any emotion now displaying feigned emotion for this interview, "Castleton Stone will be unable to produce all of the stone necessary."

"Oh?" Treacle said once more, now leaning forward on the table toward them. "And why would that be?"

Madeline studied him as intently as she could, trying to discern if he was actually surprised to hear of the issue, or if it was news to him. As far as she could tell, he was truthfully shocked by the news, although who was she to judge a man's acting ability?

Drake looked over to Madeline and nodded for her to continue.

"Our stone was vandalized."

"Vandalized?" Treacle repeated her, his shock as real as Madeline could have asked it to be.

She nodded slowly. "All of it. Really everything that was in the factory was either defaced or broken. Our stone, as you know, is made of a very dense material and is difficult to break, so whoever did this had to have known what to expect."

She looked at Treacle long and hard, but he said nothing, instead leaning back into his chair as he rubbed his chin with his thumb and index finger.

"Huh," he mused, "interesting." Then his eyes lit up and he fixed his gaze on Madeline. "And just how are the rest of your clients taking this little setback? Have their projects been affected?"

"We are working hard to replace the orders that were still on site. However, as you know, it takes time. Meanwhile, some of our other projects are on hold."

"Interesting." Treacle said, eyeing Madeline the way a vulture might when it saw its prey beginning to slow. "And does your father know about this?"

"He does not at the moment," she said, holding her head up proudly. "However, he has given me full authority to act in his stead while he is away."

"Ah, yes, away in Bath on his little tryst with your friend's mother," Treacle said, a grin spreading across his face. "Oh, don't look so shocked. Everyone knows."

"What my father chooses to do with his time is none of your business," she said, unable to hide her contempt, forgetting for a moment why they were here. Her fierce loyalty to those she loved often got the better of her. "In fact—"

Drake's hand on her arm stayed her. She was so surprised by it that she stopped talking, before embarrassment overcame her at her outburst.

"My apologies," she said, hanging her head. "I should not have—"

"No apologies necessary, Miss Castleton," Drake said lightly. "Now, back to the issue at hand. Castleton Stone has a supply issue. Is it safe to say that you were not aware of this, Treacle?"

"Of course not," he said, shaking his head. "How did it happen?"

"We do not know," Drake said, "although we would like to. Do you have any ideas as to who would do such a thing?"

Treacle looked from Drake to Madeline, obvious suspicion creeping into his gaze. "You do not think I did it, do you?"

Perhaps he was smarter than she had given him credit for.

"Would we be here presenting this to you if we did?" Drake asked, and Treacle thought over his question for a moment before shrugging.

"I suppose not." Treacle rubbed his chin again. "If I had to guess, however…"

"Yes?"

"Your factory is on land at the edge of the London Docks," he said. "Has not Hubert Powers been trying to buy the building and the land from you for some time?"

"He has," Madeline said slowly. "My father refuses to sell."

"And now your father is not here, although he still owns

the business," Treacle pointed out. "You might not have the authority to sell, but it is easier to discredit you. You are not only a woman, but new to this position of power, and you have shown poor judgement in the past."

Drake cleared his throat and shot Treacle a pointed look, but he simply shrugged and held his hands out.

"I am only stating a fact. Not trying to insult her."

Drake steadied a look at him, and it was only upon closer inspection did Madeline see that Drake's hands had curled into fists on his lap, his jaw clenched tightly as though he was holding back from what he was really wanting to say.

"He's right." Madeline said the words before she even realized she was going to, and both men swung their heads to look at her.

"Miss Castleton—" Drake began, but she held up a hand to stop his words.

"He is right," she repeated. "Powers has wanted the land for quite some time, but my father has been adamant in his refusal. Powers would like to extend the docks, to allow for his business to better serve the ships coming into the harbour. Castleton Stone would be the ideal location, but my father will not budge, no matter what Powers offers him. If our business fails, however, we would have to sell the building, and he would be right there to buy it. It would all fall into his hands."

"Maybe you are a bit more intelligent than I thought, Miss Castleton," Treacle said lazily from the other side of the table before he yawned. "None of this, however, has anything to do with me. Now, were the two of you actually here with this so-called proposal, or were you only here to question me about the vandalism in your warehouse?"

Madeline obviously did not appropriately hide her guilt, and Treacle guessed the truth before Drake could say anything otherwise.

"As I thought," he said with a smirk. "Well, as fun as this has been, I have other things to do." He stood. "Good day, Miss Castleton, Mr. Smith. As much as I would not like to see a man like Powers win, I also must tell you that I cannot wish your business success, for that only takes away from mine. Farewell."

Madeline only nodded as Drake led her down the hallway and out of the building.

CHAPTER 6

"Thank you."

Drake turned to Miss Castleton's soft voice, finding her looking up at him, with ocean-blue eyes wide beneath her white bonnet.

He cleared the gruffness from his throat.

"There's nothing to thank me for. I am only doing my job."

It was the truth. He didn't see why on earth she would thank him. He should have been firmer and convinced her to stay out of this and allow him to work alone. He could hardly imagine what she must have been thinking after all Treacle had said about her, and he felt like an utter lout that he had not been able to tell Treacle exactly what he longed to, which was for him to take his cheap shots and go straight to hell.

But then they wouldn't have gotten anywhere.

"He should never have said such things to you," Drake said, looking away from her, away from the wisps of her blond hair that had come loose and were waving around her face in the breeze.

"What happened is what happened," she said, her words

stoic. "The past cannot be changed, and if I choose to stay and live and work in London, then I must accept that people will use the scandal against me."

"The scandal was hardly your fault."

"But it was, in a way," she said softly. "I allowed it to happen. I will overcome it, though."

"Of course you will," he said, his voice hoarse. He was not overly proficient in comforting women, although he was not entirely sure that was what Madeline wished for, anyway.

"I thought he seemed surprised regarding the vandalism," she said, changing the subject slightly, relieving him.

Drake nodded. "I agree. Although it seemed he was somewhat suspicious that he would be approached for a project with Castleton Stone. Do you truly believe that Powers would ruin an entire business in order to obtain the land?"

Madeline sighed. "I have never had many dealings with him myself, although my father has never had anything particularly kind to say about him. It seems somewhat extreme just to obtain land along the Thames."

Drake placed his hands in his pockets, jingling the coins within.

"Miss Castleton…"

"Yes?"

"Have you thought about the fact that this could have been an accident? Or, perhaps, an employee who is not particularly pleased about something? An act that you will simply have to move on from?"

Madeline stared at him for a moment before beginning to shake her head, and he had the impression that he was somehow found lacking.

"You know what, Drake?" she said, ire in her tone, "You obviously feel that my little problem is not worthy of your time, so you are free to go. I will figure this out myself."

"Miss Castleton—" he began. He should have known that

she would not take his suggestion well. She interrupted him, however, before he could say anything else.

"I understand my case does not hold much importance. Except it *is* something of note — to me. I have offered you an out once before. Constable Marshall seemed more than happy to take on the job, and I would be pleased to offer it to him if he will promise to provide the time required. Now, for the last time, are you going to help me or not?"

Drake couldn't help but be surprised at her ultimatum. She seemed so fragile, and yet she had this quiet strength that surfaced now and then — a strength that he respected.

"My apologies, Miss Castleton. Never meant to offend. I'll refrain from suggesting such a thing again, although we must consider the fact that someone who works for you could have done this."

"I am aware of that, Drake, and my cousin and I are looking into it."

"Good," he said. He was not overly confident in Bennett Castleton's abilities and would therefore focus his investigation on their employees as well, but for now he would do what he could to determine if any outsiders had a hand in this. "Do you think Treacle would say anything to this Powers to warn him off?"

He looked back to Miss Castleton, who tilted her head in consideration of his question.

"I don't think so," she finally said. "He has no allegiance to him, and while he would like to see the downfall of Castleton Stone, I think he would want to see it at his own hands, and not by Powers. He wouldn't want a stone business to succumb so easily."

"Fair enough," Drake said. "I will make an appointment to see Powers. And, before you try to ask, no, you will not be coming along."

She just stared at him, and he had a feeling that even

though she had chosen not to voice her disagreement, she was going to do as she wished no matter what he said.

"Before you do so, why do you not come to the factory? I will show you more of how the stone is made and how it was vandalized. It could, perhaps, demonstrate to you that it is nearly impossible for this to have been an accident."

Drake considered her for a moment. There was much else he had to do — actions of importance that had been sent his way — but she was right. He actually should have thought of such a thing himself when she had first asked for his assistance, but he hadn't been particularly invested in the case at the time.

"Very well," he said curtly. "I shall meet you at your factory."

"Would you like to travel with me?" she asked. "I have my carriage."

"You are traveling alone?" he lifted a brow.

"Yes," she said, nodding curtly. "I had no one else to accompany me, and I am old enough to make my own decisions."

"It is not at all safe, Miss Castleton."

"I have a driver."

"Even so," he was already shaking his head, "I now have no choice but to escort you back."

"I didn't realize it would be such a hardship."

Drake lifted an eyebrow. "I must say, Miss Castleton, you have much more spark than I had guessed."

"You must bring the best out of me," she said wryly as the carriage came to a halt beside them and Drake helped her up into it, waving the driver away.

"So tell me," she said, as she sat across from him, trying to ignore the shiver of warmth that crawled through her whenever their knees brushed against one another, "how does one become a constable?"

"I asked to join," he said, looking away from her and out the window of the carriage. "It took some time, but I finally proved my worth when I captured a thief that had been targeting some of London's jewelers."

"How intriguing," she said, looking up at him, and he gathered that those blue eyes of hers caught more than she let on. "Have you always had such a sense of right and wrong, of wanting to pursue justice?"

"I suppose," he said cryptically, having no wish to tell her the full story of his past.

"What does your family think of your profession?"

"They are proud but worried at times."

"That is understandable."

She was playing with threads in her skirt's embroidery then, and Drake realized belatedly that she was simply making conversation because she was nervous, attempting to fill the silence, and he was being a cold beast about it.

"And you, Miss Castleton?" he said stiffly, polite discussion foreign to his tongue. "How does a woman become so interested in her father's stone business?"

A small, reminiscent smile played on her lips. "It has always been just my father and me," she said, her gaze faraway. "My mother died when I was young, and my father was so involved in his work that I spent a great deal of time with him, sitting in the very office that he still holds today or running around the factory, hassling the sculptors. He taught me everything about the business, and soon enough we both realized just how much I wanted to be a part of it. He is aware that it is not exactly what most young women would do with their lives, but he is supportive of my endeavor. He is, actually, supportive of anything I choose to do."

She was silent for a moment, but Drake sensed there was more she wanted to say and, like any good investigator, he waited, allowing the silence to spur on her words.

"I know he was disappointed when I married Lord Donning and was no longer able to spend time with him at the business. But he understood. When one is married to a peer, she does not work at a stone business — or any business."

"You also had plenty of problems of your own."

"Which I didn't realize until it was too late," she said, softly, looking down at her feet, and Drake couldn't help himself from reaching out and taking one of her hands in his. Hers were gloved, and yet it still felt as though her dainty, soft hand did not belong in his hardened one that had been dirtied more often than he cared to think about.

"You survived, Miss Castleton," he said. "We all do."

He dropped her hand abruptly when her eyes flew to his, apparently hearing what he didn't say — that he had survived something himself.

Fortunately, the carriage came to a halt with a jerk, but Madeline, having been looking across the carriage at him instead of out the window, was ill-prepared for the stop and went flying off the seat toward him. His hands instinctively came out to her, capturing her in his embrace.

He should have immediately set her back on the seat behind her. He should have apologized. He should have asked if she was all right.

But he did none of those things.

Her face — her beautiful face — was so close to his, her lips red and pert and entirely kissable. He bent his head, knowing that he had no business even thinking about what it would be like to feel her lips on his, to know her taste, to capture her essence. But he was unable to stop himself.

All the restraint, all of the control that led him through his life and made him proficient at what he did fled with Madeline Castleton in his arms.

"Miss Castleton—"

"Madeline."

"Madeline," he murmured, his lips now but a breath away from hers. "I—"

The carriage door opened, and Madeline flew back into her original seat.

"'ere you go, Miss Castleton. I apologize for taking so long, but I—"

The footman blinked as he looked back and forth between Madeline and Drake. They were a respectable distance apart, but her flushed face and bright eyes gave her away — gave *them* away — even though nothing at all had happened.

"Well, shall we look at the factory, then, Miss Castleton?" Drake asked, but before they were even out of the door, a figure came running up to them from the factory beyond.

"Madeline? Oh, Madeline, thank goodness!" her cousin puffed as he neared, out of breath from his short sprint. "We have been looking everywhere for you."

"I was helping Drake investigate Treacle," she said, although Drake didn't see any need for her to defend herself. "What's wrong?"

"It's the stone," Castleton said, still spitting. "We added the water to mix it, laid it out and fit it into the molds, but the formula's off. The stone won't set. It keeps cracking."

"What do you mean?" she asked, panic storming her eyes, and she took off at a run as fast as she could with her skirts restricting her, following Bennett.

Drake couldn't help but follow along, as though pulled in her wake.

She stopped so quickly that he nearly ran into the back of her, and he stepped closer, peering over her shoulder to determine what it was that had so caught her attention.

Madeline stepped past Bennett and the man who was currently working with the liquid in the vat before them, stirring it with a large stick. She held out her hand for it and then lifted and turned it so that the clay below streamed out in one long line of slop.

"This has gone through firing?" she asked the man, who seemed young, eager, and quite worried.

"Not this, ma'am," he said, "but that over there. This hasn't been molded or entered the kiln yet and we're trying to see what went wrong."

"It should be much firmer than this," she said, mostly to herself, although Drake wondered if some of it was for his benefit. "It should be hard... unbendable." She dropped the stick and walked briskly across the room. "What happened once it fired?"

"It was only in for a day before we checked it. Already it came out hard, flaky, and cracked," Bennett said, rushing over to her side. "It turns to near powder on the touch."

"What do you use to make it?" Drake asked, but Madeline was shaking her head.

"That, we cannot reveal."

"I have no one to tell," he said dryly.

"Unfortunately, Detective, I am not even privy to such information," Bennett said. "Only Madeline and her father know."

"Is this true?" Drake asked Madeline, somewhat surprised.

She nodded.

"It is the only way to ensure it can never be stolen from us. There are other companies — such as Treacle's — that have created a similar product, but none like this. We all know parts of it, but I finish it myself."

Bennett studied her. "You did finish it, did you not?"

"Of course I did," she said, lifting her chin with some apparent ire. "The last I saw it, it was like clay, ready to be molded. Not this... whatever this is."

She peered more closely at it, sniffing it.

"I believe someone stole the actual product and replaced it with what's here. This does not even resemble Castleton stone. Who was keeping watch overnight?"

"There was a... misunderstanding," Bennet said with some exasperation. "We missed appointing someone last night. It won't happen again. But until then..."

She rubbed her forehead before looking around the factory. All eyes were on her, waiting for a command from her, a decision, something to tell them just what they should all do next.

Drake noticed her lip wobble slightly — he wondered if he was the only one who did — before she caught it in her teeth and took a deep breath, seeming to come to a decision.

"Get rid of this," she commanded. "And start a new batch."

"But—" Bennett began, but she whirled around and set her eyes on him.

"What else would you have me do?" she hissed, perhaps so that others around them could not hear. "We cannot continue without any supply. We must try again."

"Only for it to be sabotaged once more?" Bennett asked, shaking his head. "Perhaps we best wait for your father to return."

She set her jaw. "We will not." She turned to the other men. "Please tell me when we are near to finishing. I shall be in my office."

Then she turned around and strode off like a queen.

Drake could only follow.

"Do you believe me now?" she asked as they entered what he guessed was Ezra Castleton's office. The walls were lined with bookshelves, but instead of holding tomes of literature, they held small sculptures that he could only assume were made of Castleton stone. A small table surrounded by four chairs sat in the corner, with a massive desk taking up the middle of the room.

Drake sighed as he eased himself back in the chair across from her desk. He did believe her, although he didn't want to readily admit it. "I suppose now I have no choice but to continue my investigation."

"You say that as though it is my fault. I would most certainly prefer to not have to deal with this."

Drake crossed his arms over his chest and leaned back. "I am not accusing you of anything at all. But obviously there was some kind of switch, and it likely happened during the middle of the night, unless all of your employees were involved with it. Would you consider that as a possibility?"

She was already shaking her head. "Absolutely not. Most of these men have been with us for years."

"I know you are loyal, Miss Castleton, but — are they?"

She was still standing, looking out the window at the yard before her, land which extended from the factory itself. He watched the long expanse of her neck as she swallowed, before leaning over completely and resting her head on the glass.

"I thought they were. But I don't seem to know anything anymore." She pressed herself backward and looked at him. "There only seems to be one person I can trust."

He lifted an eyebrow.

"Myself."

His heart and his hope inexplicably fell as he realized just what he had been hoping she would say.

"Therefore," she continued, "if anyone is going to make this right, it will be me. Now, the question is — are you going to help me or not?"

CHAPTER 7

Drake had made plans for tonight. Plans which involved the package that was currently sitting on the middle of the sole table in his small home at the edge of Covent Garden; a package waiting for him to unravel its clues.

But it would have to wait.

For Madeline Castleton was determined to stand guard over her precious stone, with or without him.

So *with* it would be.

"Why didn't you have your cousin help?" Drake asked as he joined her inside the darkened building, his voice harsh in the night, echoing off the empty vats and stone that remained, the building barren with the lack of supply.

"Bennett would be useless if he actually had to guard against any sort of attack," she said with a chuckle, and Drake was strangely warmed by her words and the obvious confidence in *him*.

"You don't have to stay here all night," he said. "I am happy to keep watch myself."

"Thank you, Drake, but I would prefer to stay."

"Don't trust me, then?"

His words were infused with his usual nonchalance, but the thought cut, though why, he had no idea.

"I trust you as much as nearly anyone," she said softly, "but I would still prefer to be here. We worked until sundown and the first shift of our workers will begin at dawn, so it will not be long before you can return home and get some sleep."

"I don't need to sleep." He actually *couldn't* sleep, but she didn't need to know the difference.

"I understand that," she said softly. "Though I'm always told that everyone needs to sleep."

"Not me," he said, his eyes having adjusted to the dark building. Windows lined the south-facing wall in one long row, admitting just enough moon and street light for him to make out the shapes within the factory, creating the scene of a frightening story one told to children to scare them away from poor behavior.

He could also see Madeline. Her hair glinted near silver in the darkness, her dress tonight dark and narrow, hardly discernible.

"Shall we find somewhere more comfortable to wait?"

"There are some chairs along the far wall," she said, her voice seemingly untethered as she weaved her way around the floor, as though she was dancing solo, the pieces of equipment other couples. "We could sit there. I also had a mind to do some patrolling around the building."

"Quite the detective yourself, aren't you?"

He noted her head turn as she looked toward him over her shoulder. He couldn't detect her expression, but he guessed it was one of disdain. She did not seem to take all too kindly to his teasing.

When she answered him, however, there was mirth in her words.

"Well, if this business does not work out for me, it is good to know that I have a second career option."

"You could also marry," he suggested. "'Tis what most women do."

"I tried that already," she said, her words now harsh. "It did not work out particularly well for me."

"Another man might be different."

"He might," she said, her voice, with her head turned away from him, nearly lost in the void. "But he might not. And that is not a chance I am willing to take."

A sudden need to throttle Kurt Maxfeld for how deeply he had hurt this woman overcame Drake to the point that he was clenching and unclenching his fists as he walked. The man had broken Madeline Castleton's spirit, and Drake wondered how it could ever be put back together again.

He also wondered why it mattered to him so much.

Must be his penchant to find justice for victims and all that.

For no other reason was possible. That part of him — the part that might care for others, or search for connection beyond those who had been wronged — was closed off, never to be awoken again.

For it hurt too much. His emotions were best left where they were — dormant.

Suddenly Madeline whirled around and looked at him.

"Did you see that?" she whispered loudly.

"See what?"

He had been daydreaming, and because of it, he had obviously missed something important. Something even Madeline had seen.

"There was a shadow over by the window," she said as she inched back farther into the darkness next to him.

"A shadow?" he asked, furrowing his brow. "I hardly think so, I—"

But there it was again. The light from the window was blocked, just for a moment.

He sensed rather than saw Madeline shiver next to him.

"Let's move," he said, his instincts and training taking over as he drew her back against the wall. But she was the one who knew the building, and she quickly wriggled out of his grasp, although she took his hand and began leading him along the outskirts of the large room.

"Back here," she whispered. "We'll be able to see everything and be hidden from view."

Drake was actually shocked that there was anything of note happening tonight. But quite truthfully, he had not thought that they would actually stumble across anything of note tonight.

Perhaps he was wrong. Or… there was the possibility that Madeline had staged this for him. Why she would do such a thing, he had no idea, but he had seen stranger situations.

They stopped behind a sculpture of a siren reclining on a stone that was still intact and was, as far as he was aware, part of the dwindling stock that Madeline and Castleton Stone had remaining.

Madeline was right. From here, the entire factory stretched out before them, but they would be well concealed back in this corner.

He stepped into the small recess between the mermaid and the wall and then reached out a hand for Madeline to join him, but the fit was tight, and by the time she worked herself between the wall and the stone, as slim as she was, there was still hardly room for the two of them.

She wiggled and he inched forward and back, until finally the only way he could find a place of comfort for both of them was to lift his arm up and then place it around her so that it was draped over her chest, drawing her back in toward him.

"Sorry," he muttered in her ear, although the apology was just as much to himself as to her, for he was having difficulty thinking straight with her pressed up against him as she was.

It had been too long since a woman had been close to him like this, too long since anyone had made him feel or think about anything other than the job or the mission he had vowed to fulfill.

She was just a slip of a woman, and yet she was powerfully drawing him in.

Which he did not like. Not one bit.

Regain control, Drake.

He took a deep breath, his filling chest expanding against her back, and she went rigid before him. Well, if she was uncomfortable, it was her own fault. She had insisted on coming here with him tonight.

He was sure she was regretting her decision now.

* * *

Madeline closed her eyes as the wall of Drake's hard, muscled chest pushed against her back, even as she could feel the beat of his heart *pum-pumming* against her.

Slower than her own heartbeat, which was racing like the beat of the hooves of a horse pulling a curricle racing to Brighton on a Sunday.

Drake didn't even want her here, she reminded herself. To him, being pressed up against a woman like her was obviously of no consequence. She was sure a man such as he, so dark and mysterious, likely took pleasure in women with generous curves and large breasts and experienced in seduction fighting for his attentions.

She would never have caught his eye if it wasn't for her pocketbook and her case.

Why was she spending even a moment considering a man who apparently had no emotions of his own to speak of?

Because of his body, so hard and lean against her.

Because of his eyes, dark and hooded and hiding what she was sure were all sorts of secrets.

Because of his proximity, here in the darkness, providing safety where just on the other side of this stone lurked the enemy.

Because he had ultimately proven himself to be the one person she could trust.

If it wasn't for him, she would be here, alone, paralyzed by her fear of how to best approach the situation.

But he was here, and because of that, she would be safe. She didn't know how she was so sure of it, but she was.

The door, far across the building, creaked open, nearly silent, but the light emitted by the action gave it away.

A figure slipped in — just one, as far as Madeline could tell. She craned her neck to better see, and as she did, Drake's breath tickled the skin behind her ear and she shivered involuntarily once more.

She couldn't make out, however, who had entered and nor, apparently, could Drake by the way he was craning his neck behind her. She could see that the man was nearing the vats where they had begun to remake the formula for the stone. Much of it was only missing the ingredients that only she knew to include.

"Do you recognize him?" Drake murmured in her ear, and she shook her head.

"Too far," she whispered.

"Stay here," he said, pressing his other hand against her hip, as though he could keep her in one place by doing so. "I'm going to see if I can get a better look."

He retrieved his arm, and Madeline was lost for a moment by its sudden absence. She remained rooted to the spot as she watched him begin to inch his way over to the new arrival, taking a moment to stop behind various instruments, supplies, and product as he neared.

Madeline hesitated for a moment before she began to follow, holding up her skirts so that they wouldn't swish and draw attention toward them.

A flicker of light came on, as the occupant seemed to have lit a lantern in order to find his way around. Perfect. Maybe then they would be able to see his face — for that, she could tell. This was most certainly a he.

Just then a sound came from the door, and all three of them in the building jerked their heads up to see.

It sounded like... a whistle? Madeline narrowed her eyes. It was a familiar whistle. But where had she... the door opened and the whistling of a merry tune grew in volume. A lantern was raised at the door, and she saw... Bennett?

Madeline clapped a hand over her mouth to keep her exclamation from making any noise. What was her cousin doing here? He couldn't be part of this — could he? He was the most loyal of anyone she knew. What she couldn't help, however, was her stumble backward. Her foot caught an errant piece of stone, rubble from the vandalism, and she nearly went flying back into the pile behind her, just managing to catch herself before she went down.

She did, however, make a great deal of noise as she saved herself.

"I say!" Bennett exclaimed, his eyes finding her. "Who is there?" He lifted the lantern as he neared, allowing light to flood the room. "Madeline? What is happening here?"

She was rendered speechless for a moment, until a sharp crack came from the side of the room where the initial intruder had been, while at nearly the same time she was launched sideways, her body involuntarily turning at the last moment so that she landed on something soft and comfortable that broke her fall.

She opened her eyes to find Drake's dark ones running up and down her face before searching her body below.

"Are you hurt?" he asked, gruffly and quickly. She shook her head.

"Good. Let's go," he said, and then before she knew what was happening, he grabbed her hands, pulled her up, and was leading her out of the building through the back door. Her strides were much shorter than his, but she tried to churn her legs quickly to keep up.

"What's happening?" she asked, her voice coming in quick puffs.

"We were shot at, that's what's happening," he said, his voice dourly, their sprint out of the factory not seeming to have any impact on his breath. "Hurry, before we are followed."

"But what about Bennett?" she asked, worried that her cousin might be caught in the line of fire.

"He's on his own," Drake said grimly. "I can only protect one of you, and I choose you."

"Because I am the job," she said wryly as she continued to follow him down the dark street, the sound of the Thames on the other side of the buildings guiding them along.

He cast a look over his shoulder at her, but she couldn't make out his expression in the darkness of the night.

Another shot rang out from behind them, and Madeline couldn't help her exclamation as she tried to run even faster, but her lungs, weakened from the poisoning earlier in the year, couldn't seem to match her determination, no matter how hard she tried.

She looked back over her shoulder, but nearly ran into the side of the building in the process. Drake reached out an arm and righted her before whispering harshly, "In here!"

and then propelled her into an alleyway. He stopped within an alcove that was the entrance to another building, pressing her up against the door so that he could step in after her, his body holding her hostage.

His breath was now ragged in her ear, and she was glad to see that some level of physical exertion affected him. She had been beginning to wonder whether he was actually human or not.

"Don't move," he commanded urgently, and she rolled her eyes, even though he couldn't see them. As if she had any choice but to stay still, from how intently he had her trapped against the door.

For a moment, a sense of panic overcame her, and a flood of memories rushed back — of how the drug Maxfeld had given her kept her weighed down on the bed, nearly unable to move by the end of it. She had been so helpless, lying there, alone, with no hope of recovery — her options had been to die by poisoning or by starvation.

Until, thankfully, Alice had come for her.

She was safe now, she knew that, but there were moments, like this one, where she was taken back to that feeling of helplessness — the feeling that she never wanted to experience again.

But then Drake's head dipped, and he was in her ear, his voice surprisingly soothing.

"It's all right," he said, and Madeline was instantly ashamed that she had allowed her discomfort to be so obvious. "We'll be back into the alley, into the freedom of the night air, in moments. We just have to let him pass, to keep both of us safe."

She nodded into his shoulder.

"Deep breaths," he said again. "Deep breaths."

Madeline did as he said, and her senses were filled with

the smell of him — a hint of coffee that hung on the fabric of his jacket. He must drink it often.

She tilted her head back to ask him, just as he bent his head to her. All she could see were his lips before her, and she wondered, what would it be like to kiss him? Would his lips be hard and unrelenting, or would they be soft and forgiving, the side that he showed her now and again?

She no longer had a chance to consider it, however, for one of his hands wrapped around the back of her head, and he touched his forehead to hers.

"Can I kiss you?" he asked, the question surprising and his voice hushed in the darkness that had become near silent despite the noise she knew accompanied every London night.

She nodded, tilting her head back ever so slightly, just enough to allow his lips to descend on hers.

As it turned out, they were somewhere in between — firm yet gentle, exploring yet thoughtful. Madeline had only been kissed by one other man before — the only man she had ever thought she would kiss — and while she had enjoyed it, at least at first, this was different. *This* was nothing short of magic.

For Drake's kiss was more giving, more contemplative, more understanding of what she needed and what she was ready for at this particular moment.

So it surprised her that when he finally broke away, he leaned back and looked down at her with eyes that were far more confused than she felt.

"Madeline," he said, his voice husky, "I—"

"I say, you there!"

"Bennett!" she exclaimed as Drake stepped back and away from her. "Thank goodness you're all right."

She was happy to see her cousin apparently unscathed,

although she couldn't help the slight twinge of irritation at his timing. What had Drake been about to say?

"Madeline, what happened in there?" he asked, his lantern swinging wildly. "And what is *he* doing here?"

"Drake?" she asked, turning her head to look at him. "I asked him to help me keep a look out in the factory tonight. What were you doing there?"

"Me?" Bennett asked, splaying a hand across his heart as Drake quietly watched them both, arms crossed over his chest — a chest that Madeline could hardly believe she had been snug against just moments ago. "I was doing exactly that — coming to ensure all was well and that no one was further messing with the inventory."

Madeline sighed, dropping her hands. Bennett always meant well.

"We should have discussed it," she said. "Then we would not have gotten in one another's way."

"Did you see the intruder?" Drake asked, his deep, raspy voice at odds with Bennett's.

"I didn't see anything," Bennett said, hanging his head somewhat shamefully. "In truth, I didn't see that anything was amiss until I heard the shot ring out. I suppose that is why you are the detective and I am part of a stone-making company."

He laughed wryly, and Madeline couldn't help but shrug one shoulder.

"Well, thank you, Bennett, for trying, and thank goodness none of us were hurt. I just wish we had seen who it was."

"I'll have another detective come and watch the factory for the rest of the night while I see you home, Miss Castleton," Drake said, and Bennett held up a hand.

"I can certainly look after my cousin."

"I must insist," Drake said. "I have a weapon, if necessary."

"Then why didn't you use it?" Bennett asked wryly.

"I was more concerned with seeing your cousin to safety," Drake said, his voice dry with obvious displeasure at being so questioned.

"Yes, yes, very good," Bennett finally said, dropping his arms as relief flooded through Madeline that he was no longer pressing Drake. "Well, I will go watch over the factory until you send someone else."

"Thank you, Bennett," Madeline said, wanting to soften Drake's censure. Bennett really had been trying his best. "Goodnight."

CHAPTER 8

What had he been thinking?

Drake sat at the writing table in his small study, replaying the night's events as he stared down at the package in front of him.

He opened up the box, carefully untying the twine first to reveal the contents within as his mind wandered to earlier this evening.

If there was anything he should be carefully reviewing, it was what had happened in the factory. He had been so close to catching the intruder. If only Madeline's most unhelpful cousin hadn't walked in when he did.

But instead, all Drake could think about was his kiss with her. He should never have done it, of that he was well aware. He couldn't accurately explain just what had convinced him that it was the right thing to do. Perhaps it was their proximity, her lips so close to his. She was a beautiful woman, of that there was no denying. There was something more, however… it could have been her vulnerability. She had opened herself up to him, allowed him to see that the circumstances had overwhelmed her. He had been honored that she had let him in, had listened to his words, had allowed them to calm her.

He had an innate sense of pride that he had been able to comfort her. He was not exactly the comforting type, but she seemed to respond to him.

Right before he had kissed her, he had remembered all she had been through, had realized that she was basically at his mercy, as trapped as she was by his body — and so he had asked for her permission. And had been so gratified and relieved when she had said yes.

It was everything he could have asked for, and yet he wished it had never happened. For now, he wanted nothing more than to do it again.

But he couldn't. For that could lead to more, and more—right now—was not possible. Nor would it likely ever be.

Not with this in front of him.

A clue, at last, one for which he had been searching for over so many years now, the entire reason why he had dedicated his life to the search for truth and justice.

It was what had carried him on after a near-silent carriage ride home with Madeline, after he had left her at the door and continued on here, to his own residence.

It seemed rather ordinary. A satchel.

But his breath caught as his fingers touched the worn leather and he lifted it out to set it in front of him. It was so much more than just a satchel.

He would know this anywhere. It was his father's. Whoever had sent this to him knew what happened to his parents. They had to. It was ripped, aged, smelled musty and not at all like the leather and parchment scent of his father that he still remembered.

But it was his. Drake was sure of it.

And then there was what was inside. The bundle of notes that was more money than Drake would make in a year as a detective. Had it been his father's? Or was someone attempting some restitution for taking Drake's parents from him?

He didn't want to believe any ill about his parents, but the date on the notes told him that these were not new... they must have been earned years prior. Years around when he had lost his parents.

He sighed, running his hands through his hair.

Where did he go from here? He had decided years ago that he would leave this alone, that there was no mystery to solve, that he would let it go and would focus instead on righting the wrongs he could control, for the people who were still waiting for their answers and their vengeance.

But now, with this... it told him that there was *someone* out there who knew what had happened. There was a reason Drake was a detective, and now was the time he had to use all of his reasoning to determine the heart of the matter.

He lifted the satchel again, the soft leather brushing against his hands like a second skin. He ran his fingers over the outside of it, where the leather had nearly worn off. But there... what was that? There was a lump of some sort. Was it a defect in the leather? No...

There was something there. Something within. Drake's heart began to beat rapidly as he realized, if he could only still his fingers long enough to search within, he might find something that would provide him answers, if nothing else.

He opened the satchel, his shaking hands nearly pulling the fabric apart in his quest to find whatever it was that was calling him.

There. It was barely noticeable, so well it had been stitched, but then, his mother had always been an excellent seamstress. He nearly tore the fabric apart, but then realized that doing so would destroy one of the only things he had left from his parents, an unexpected gift.

He looked around the room, his eyes lighting on the letter opener. He carefully worked it into the stitching, breaking it stitch by stitch until the satchel was open to him, and finally, there, within, was a small pendant.

Drake lifted out the circle, turning it around within his fingers, holding it up to the candle that was already wearing down next to him.

It looked like it was some kind of bird — a hawk perhaps? He was no ornithologist, that was for certain, but he wondered what the significance of it was.

Something about it seemed familiar to him, but he could not determine just where he had seen it before.

He would take it to Bow Street tomorrow. Maybe someone there would recognize it.

He could only hope.

* * *

THE FIRST THING Madeline did the next morning was review her correspondence to ensure that all had been well at the factory since she had left it last night.

It had been.

The second thing she did was greet her aunt, who had already eaten in her room and was now sitting in front of the fire with a book in hand — where she spent most of her days. Besides the dinner hour, when she was always interested in hearing Madeline's activities of the day, this was where she could usually be found.

Third, she sent a note to Alice, requesting a visit. She desperately needed to speak to someone, and who else than her very closest of friends, who would understand better than anyone the conundrum she faced?

And so it was that two hours later she found herself on the doorstep of what had once been the Dorrington London

House, but was now the home of Alice and Benjamin Luxington. Benjamin's brother, now Lord Dorrington, had no wish to reside there after the death of his father and had gifted his house to Benjamin.

"Madeline!" Alice practically squealed as she opened the door and welcomed her.

Alice was never one for much formality, and she gave Madeline such a squeeze that she let out an "oomph."

"Sorry," Alice said with a bit of a bashful smile. "It's just been some time now, and I am so happy to see you. I find myself at home far too often, what with feeling rather ill since I began expecting."

"Well, you look better than you ever have," Madeline said, with all truthfulness. Alice had always been beautiful, but now she was practically glowing.

"As do you," Alice said, but Madeline waved a hand in the air, well aware that Alice was just being kind. She knew she was still so wan that she looked rather sickly and she had become far too thin. Which was why she had been shocked that Drake would have any inkling to come close to her, let alone to kiss her.

"Now," Alice said as she perched on the edge of one of the red parlor chairs and settled her skirts around her legs. The sun was beautiful today, shining in through the glass panes to reflect on Alice as though she was a goddess.

Madeline moved over on the sofa to allow the sun to more thoroughly warm her back.

"Tell me all that has happened. Have you determined who is sabotaging you? Has Drake been of any help? What do you think, is he not strikingly handsome?"

Madeline laughed at the barrage of questions, holding up a hand to stop her friend.

"Which question would you like answered first?" she

asked, but before Alice could respond, there was a knock at the door and the butler soon showed in another woman.

"Rose!" Alice exclaimed, standing to greet the young woman who stood at the entryway, a warm though somewhat hesitant smile on her face. "What are you doing here? I didn't know you were in London!"

"I'm back for a short visit," Rose said, following Alice into the room and sitting next to Madeline on the sofa. "I apologize. I didn't realize I would be interrupting."

"Not at all," Alice said, shaking her head. "Do you remember Madeline?"

"Of course," Rose said with a nod of her head. Madeline had met her briefly at Alice's wedding, and while she seemed quite lovely, Madeline was somewhat embarrassed, for she was aware that Rose had been privy to her situation last year.

Rose was an interesting woman herself. Madeline was aware that Rose had discovered the bones of a previously unknown creature on the shores of her hometown of Lyme, and a woman with such intelligence must think her a fool.

"How are you?" Rose asked her now, and when she looked at her, her dark-brown eyes full of care and concern, Madeline's worry over her supposed judgment lessened some.

"I am well now," Madeline said truthfully.

"We have a new mystery!" Alice pronounced, and then proceeded to tell Rose all that had been occurring at Madeline's factory.

"How very interesting," Rose murmured. "What do you suppose to do about it?"

"We have one of the finest detectives on the case," Alice said. "I'm not sure if you remember Drake from the wedding."

"I do," Rose said, nodding. "He is a hard man to miss."

"That is what I was just saying!" Alice exclaimed. "So tell us, Madeline. What is it like working with him?"

"He is…" she struggled, unsure of how much to say. While she was not afraid of sharing her thoughts with Alice, nor even Rose, it was as though putting her attraction to him out into the world somehow made it more real. Her face must have given her away though, for Alice interrupted her musings with an "Aha!"

"What?" Madeline asked, taken aback.

"You *feel* something for him."

"I do not!" Madeline protested, even though it seemed that she very much did. "He is… intriguing, yes, but I do not consider him at all beyond the assistance he is providing."

"No?" Alice arched an eyebrow, and Madeline dipped her head. She didn't want to keep anything from Alice, and yet—

"Although there was an… incident."

"Oh?"

"We were at the factory last night — that is an entirely different part to this story — and he, well… he kissed me."

"Oh!" Alice's hands flew to her cheeks as her mouth rounded into an O. One could always count on Alice to provide the most appropriate reactions. "He did? How was it? How did it start? What was it like?"

Madeline chuckled at the questions again. "It was… somewhat unexpected, although he did ask permission, which I more than appreciated. And it was… nice. Sweet, actually, which I never would have supposed."

It also had a twinge of passion, but Madeline decided to keep that to herself.

"How delightful," Alice said, tilting her head to the side with a dreamy smile.

Madeline narrowed her eyes at her. "You were hoping for something like this, weren't you?"

"No—"

"Alice, it was a lovely kiss, but nothing is going to come of it."

Alice's smile dipped somewhat. "How can you be so sure?"

"Because... because there will never be a man for me. After everything that happened with Steph— Kurt Maxfeld, I have realized that my own feelings are not to be trusted. My intuition is not to be trusted. I know that I am an intelligent woman, but apparently only when it comes to numbers and ledgers, not when it comes to actually dealing with people. Which is likely precisely why I am also in the situation I am in regarding the business. For businesses are more than ledgers and accounting. It is about relationships. About developing trust and loyalty, with which I have clearly struggled."

"Oh, Madeline, that is not at all true."

"You are just saying that because you are my friend."

"I am not your friend."

They both swiveled their heads to the side to look at Rose, who had been sitting in silence listening to their conversation.

"At least, I am not your friend yet, although I would like to be," she smiled softly. "You seem like a wonderful woman, Madeline, and I would very much like to get to know you better. However, from what I can tell so far, you are quite intelligent, and you have a tenacity that few possess. Why, if you didn't, you would have succumbed to the situation that you were left in. You would allow your business to fail without fighting for it. But, even though you may not outwardly be as... assertive as some others—"

"Like me," Alice said with a sigh.

"Yes, like Alice," Rose said with a nod and a smile. "That doesn't mean that you do not hold the qualities of someone who can come through the darkness and emerge into the light on the other side."

Madeline allowed the words to resonate deep within her.

She appreciated them more than Rose would ever know, and yet, she wasn't sure if she was quite ready to accept whether there might be any truth to them.

"Thank you," she said softly.

"So, does that mean that you will see if you can make something with Drake?"

Madeline laughed softly. If there was ever a definition of tenacity, it could certainly be summed up in Alice.

"I don't think so," she said quietly. "I will fight for the business, but I cannot risk allowing my heart to open like that again. For if I do, and if I am broken or rejected once more… I'm not sure that I would ever be able to recover."

They were all silent for a moment, the other women apparently understanding the truth to her words.

"Very well," Alice said softly. "I understand. But just… do not turn your back on happiness forever — can you promise that?"

Madeline wasn't sure she could.

"I promise that I will try."

It was the best she could do.

CHAPTER 9

"Drake, how lovely to see you! And so soon after your last visit!"

Drake smiled, although he was somewhat vexed. He should do a better job of being there for his aunt and uncle. That they would be shocked by two visits within just over a week said something about the lack of time he spent with them.

"Stay for dinner?" his aunt asked, a spark of hope gleaming in her eyes as she wrung her hands together.

"Of course," he said, never saying no to a meal cooked by his aunt. Not only was it the best he ever ate, but he knew how much it meant to her, to ensure that he was well fed.

"Good, good," she said, before she bustled off to the kitchen, leaving Drake alone with his uncle.

"Well?" his Uncle Andrew said, eyeing him with his intense stare from within his weathered face. "Out with it. Why are you here?"

"I wanted to see you."

His uncle raised one of his generous eyebrows, not needing to say anything else.

"Fine," Drake said with a sigh. "I needed to ask you about something. I'm just not sure how."

His uncle leaned forward, the chair creaking as his weight shifted and he settled his elbows on the tops of his thighs. "If there is one thing I hope I have taught you, Drake, it is how to be straightforward and forthright. Now, tell me what's on your mind, son."

The honorific was not lost on Drake, who mulled it over in his mind as he considered his Uncle Andrew and how to put the question to him. His uncle and his father—brothers—had always been close, and his uncle had nearly been as lost as Drake after his father's death. But Uncle Andrew was right. There was only one way to approach this.

"It is about my parents."

Andrew let out an audible exhale as he pushed himself back against the chair. "What about them?"

"About their death."

His uncle shook his head slowly. "You just won't let it go, will you?"

"I tried to," Drake said, throwing up his hands, as exasperated as his uncle was. "But just when I think I'm able to move on, I'm called back to it, again and again."

"Drake," his uncle said, his voice hard, gruff, serious. "Enough. It's finished. Your parents are gone. Let them rest in peace."

Drake stared at his uncle in shock, the wall around his heart hardening. "How can you say that?" he asked, hearing the ache in his voice and swallowing it back down. "He was your brother."

"He was," Andrew said. "But he's gone. People come and people go, Drake. Don't ruin your life chasing after what you might never find."

"Uncle," Drake said, not listening to his words, refusing to allow them to enter into his consciousness, "do you know anything about what happened to them?"

"Let it go, Drake."

"But Uncle—"

"Drake."

His aunt stood in the doorframe between the kitchen and the small drawing room. Her face was drawn, her eyes sad.

"Andrew and I… we are just worried for you. We do not want to see you hurt. We want to see you live a full life, a life in which you find someone you love. Have children. Start a family. Work hard. Be happy. Do it for your parents."

The thought of a woman, of a wife, a family, sent an image of Madeline into his mind. It must have been because that was what she had wanted in life. She had thought she had found the man for her, and then it had all been taken away from her, as well as nearly her life along with it.

He wondered if she would ever trust in love again, would ever try for what she had obviously wanted, or if she had propelled all of that love into her business.

Drake sighed as he looked back and forth, between his aunt's pleading face and his uncle's set, resolute one, knowing he was not going to get anywhere with them. Yet his intuition told him, deep within, that they did know something. They just didn't want to tell him. Why, he had no idea, but he had the sense that this concern was more than the two of them watching out for him. They didn't want him to find the truth.

But he wouldn't stop until he did.

* * *

Madeline clutched the letter between her fingers as she practically ran to the study in her home to open it. She had been desperately waiting for another letter from her father, and here it was.

She had been rather vague when writing him, not wanting to worry him while he was away for the first time in what had been years. Her poor father. As much as Madeline had been through, he had been through it all with her.

Ezra Castleton was more than a typical father to Madeline; he was her mother, too. Everything he did was either for Madeline, or for the business, and finally he was doing something for himself.

She would not ruin that for him.

She found the letter opener and hastily slid it beneath the seal.

My Darling Madeline,

I am glad to hear that you are keeping well. I knew that the business would be in good hands with you. In fact, I am sure it will thrive in your care. While I understood your desire to leave Castleton Stone behind in order to marry and start a family, I am hopeful that in the future it means as much to you as it does to me.

We are doing well here in Bath. I know that you all must be scandalized to know that I am not here alone, but I have news for you — news that I can hardly wait to share. I shall leave you in suspense as I cannot wait to see the expression on your face when I tell you.

Madeline could practically hear her father's laughter at that — laughter she missed. Nobody laughed as good of a full-bodied, deep-belly laugh as did Ezra.

I shall likely be home within a fortnight. I look forward to seeing you, Madeline. I do not like being parted from you for so long.

And Madeline, after everything that happened, please continue to chase your dreams and do what makes you happy. Do not allow that good-for-nothing to change your life. You deserve all of the happiness in the world, and I pray that you do not lose your joy.

Sending you all my love,
Father

Tears pricked at Madeline's eyes as she placed the letter down on the table before her. Oh, how she missed him. He had only been gone three weeks now, and there were still another two weeks to go.

On the other hand, she had two weeks to determine just what was happening with the business. She was determined to have it solved before her father returned, to prove that his faith in her was justified.

She sat down to return her father's letter, but saw that the tray of additional correspondence was sitting next to her on the desk. She had been so involved in his letter that she had missed it.

Madeline noted familiar handwriting on a slip of paper.

Madeline, your presence is requested / required for a dinner at our home tomorrow evening at seven o'clock. Wear your pink gown. ~ Alice

Madeline was smiling as she read it, until she considered Alice's words. Why would she tell her what to wear? Unless… Alice was up to something. She sighed as she shook her head. Her friend needed to understand that she was happy. Happy with the business. Happy living her life. Happy not requiring anyone else.

All of which she would tell her when she saw her next. But she would still enjoy the dinner. She was somewhat lonely without her father. Her aunt was lovely but did not make for the most scintillating of company. One thing was for certain. Whatever Alice had in mind, it would not be boring.

* * *

DRAKE PUSHED through the heavy wooden doors of Bow Street's Magistrate Court, indecision in his heart and on his mind.

His aunt and uncle were likely right about moving on and enjoying life. But he couldn't. Not until he knew the truth.

He nodded his greeting to the clerk who sat at the front desk directing people who arrived with their concerns. Marshall was there as he always was. The man didn't seem to do much unless he was told to. He preferred to wait until he was summoned out to the country, where he would hope to be well compensated for his efforts.

The woman who sat near the front of the office gave him a nod. She was dressed in a non-descript navy dress, one that was carefully selected so as not to attract attention — which was exactly the point of her being there.

Upon entering the building, most questioned her presence, although they soon accepted that she was an assistant of some sort. It didn't seem to be the proper place for a woman, but they could understand it.

If only they knew the truth.

For Georgina Jenkins was not at all what she appeared to be.

Drake nodded to her as he walked by. They had always gotten on well, and he considered her to be as close a friend as any he had now.

"Afternoon, Georgie."

"Afternoon, yourself."

"Anyone come in today with anything interesting?"

"You think I would tell you if they did?"

"No." He shook his head. "You would keep them for yourself. You always do."

Georgina Jenkins was a constable as much as any of the rest of them. She would never go in the record books or be recorded on any roster. But there were times when a woman could do things that a man could not, and she had proven herself useful many times over.

"Say, Georgie," he said, leaning against the wall beside her, "have you ever seen anything like this before?"

He pulled the pendant out of his pocket, letting it lie flat against his palm as he held it out to her.

She tilted her head to study it.

"It's a hawk," she said.

"I know."

"I have seen it before… makes me think of something down at the docks. A business maybe?"

He shrugged. "Maybe."

Marshall ambled over. "What do you have there?" he asked.

Drake didn't think he'd be any help but showed him anyway. Marshall squinted as he peered at it.

"I've seen it before, too," he said. "I think it's from one of the gangs near the Thames."

"A gang?" he repeated, his words a hallow echo. What would his father have been doing with a gang pendant? "Are you sure?"

"Pretty sure," Marshall said with a shrug. "But it was from quite some time ago. I've seen the symbol but not a pendant like that in a long time. The new ones have changed slightly. Those belonged to the originals of the club. Most of them are gone now. Not a business that begets a long life."

Drake could only stare at it, so small in his hand. Had his father stolen it from someone? Gotten in between the wrong people? His father had been a builder, like his uncle. They had worked together, side by side, so surely his uncle would have known what his father had been involved in? Or perhaps not… he couldn't be sure.

Drake sighed and ran a hand through his hair.

"Thank you, Marshall, Georgie."

"Where's it from?" Marshall asked, but Drake ignored him and continued on to check for correspondence, only to be distracted by a missive that awaited. He looked at the back of it, surprised to find that he had been invited to dinner by Benjamin and Alice Luxington. He didn't exactly have time to go, but he also appreciated the invitation. If he said no to this there might never be another.

He scrawled his reply.

CHAPTER 10

Madeline never quite knew what to expect at one of Alice's dinner parties.

Her friend had an active imagination, which had led to her becoming one of the finest novelists in all of England.

But it also often led to her own notions on how her friends should achieve their own happily ever afters — even if they didn't want to.

At least not anymore.

Madeline had the sense that she was going to be walking into a scene of some sort, in which she was to play the heroine, with a young gentleman cast in the role of prince and savior.

Well, she would have to smile her way through it and then say farewell at the end of the night.

"I wonder who else is here."

Bennett was beside her. He had been invited along with Madeline, although she wondered just why Alice had thought to ask him. She likely felt that Madeline could use someone to look out for her, and the sad truth was, she didn't really have anyone else.

She loved her cousin, she truly did, but he was almost *too* overbearing. He played the role of protector to such an extent that it almost became difficult to breathe when he was around.

If only her father were here. He never forgot her strengths.

The door swung open and the butler welcomed her, looking behind her into the empty space — likely for her chaperone, though none would be found there. Her aunt only cared about her actions to the extent that she was interested with the tales she brought home. Besides that, Madeline was now cast into a role that really had no precedent.

She was unmarried, but ruined through no fault of her own. She had been accepted as a member of society for a small point in time, but then had been quickly dismissed when it was revealed that not only was Lord Donning a fraud, but so had been their marriage.

"Madeline!" Alice rose to greet her, catching her in an embrace. While Benjamin was the son of a marquess and Alice the daughter of a baron, meaning each of them possessed noble blood, they were commoners now — which, they both admitted, they rather enjoyed.

Madeline looked over Alice's shoulder to see just who else filled the drawing room. There was Rose Ellis, here once more. There were Lord and Lady Essex, Alice's brother and sister-in-law, and one of Lady Essex's friends and her husband, Mr. and Mrs. Archie Thompkins.

Madeline breathed a sigh of relief. No other single men. No knights-in-shining-armor. Perfect. She could relax and enjoy herself.

"I apologize for my tardiness."

Madeline closed her eyes at the voice from behind her.

It wasn't just the fact that he was there that bothered her.

No. It was the way hearing him, sensing him there, sent a flutter of tingles from the back of her neck, down her shoulders and into her stomach.

"Drake!" Alice said, moving away from Madeline before gripping her arm and propelling her around to face him. "I'm so glad you could make it. Madeline herself just arrived."

"Miss Castleton," he said with a slight bow, although something danced behind his eyes, something Madeline couldn't quite make out. He looked over at her cousin. "Mr. Castleton."

The rest of the party greeted them, although Madeline did her best to avoid Drake for most of the evening before the dinner actually began. She had spoken with him enough, had she not? What else was there to say, besides to ask him just when he was going to determine who was after Castleton Stone?

But when they went in to dinner, she found, her heart sinking, that Alice had placed placards on the tables so that she was sitting right next to him, with Bennett across the table at the very end, likely so that he couldn't interfere in her conversations with Drake. Of course. Madeline shot Alice a glance telling her exactly what she thought of the situation, but Alice took a sip of her drink and looked up to the ceiling, pretending not to notice.

Rose, at least, seemed sympathetic to her plight.

"Switch with me?" Madeline whispered to her as Rose took her seat beside her, but the young woman laughed lightly as she shook her head.

"I wouldn't want to catch Alice's ire or else it will be me next time," she murmured. "Except I'm not sure that I would turn my nose up at this one. He *is* rather handsome."

Madeline risked a glance over at Drake. Rose was right. He was handsome — too handsome. And striking. And everything that drew her, which were all the reasons for her to run far away.

After this dinner, at least.

"How are you, Madeline?" Lady Essex asked with a gentle smile, which Madeline forced herself to return. She knew the baroness actually *did* care how she was, but she also didn't love being the center of attention of all the table, particularly when they were all aware of just why that would be so.

"Very well, thank you," she said, infusing more confidence than she actually felt into her words. "My only issue now is that someone seems to be after my business, and I cannot figure out who that might be."

"Is Drake not helping you?" Alice asked innocently, and Madeline nodded before looking sideways at him.

"We are... *slowly* working on things," she said, hoping that she could, perhaps, spur him into further action.

"We are," he agreed, arching an eyebrow at her. "In fact, we will be speaking with Hubert Powers tomorrow." He gazed out toward the rest of the table. "He's the man trying to take over all of the land adjacent to the Thames, where Castleton Stone resides."

Suddenly Drake had become rather chatty.

"Do you really think it could be him?" Mr. Thompkins asked, and Madeline just shrugged.

"I suppose we shall find out tomorrow, then."

"Ah..." Drake held up a finger as the first course was served. Alice's dinners might not have been nearly as extravagant as a typical *ton* dinner, but they were an event in their own right. "By *we*, Miss Castleton, I meant one of my associates and me. I think you have had enough adventure."

Madeline stilled. "I'm so sorry?"

"I have put you in danger enough through the course of this investigation," he said, lower now, so that the conversation was between the two of them and not the entire table, although they all seemed to notice the tension between them that instantly arose. "I will go see him, and I will be sure to advise you of all that I find out."

"I can be of help."

"We shall discuss it later," Drake said, although Madeline knew what that meant. It meant that he was going to do as he pleased and ignore her wants completely.

She felt like grunting her frustration, but Benjamin Luxington, Alice's husband, who had become rather friendly with Drake last year, caught Drake's attention before she could make her chagrin known.

Drake leaned over toward him, but despite Benjamin's low tone, Madeline heard snippets of the conversation.

She most certainly heard Drake's response.

"What?" he almost roared, and the entire table turned toward him. "My apologies," he said, looking around at the rest of them. "I overreacted."

"He what?" she heard him insist to Benjamin. "When? How?"

Benjamin murmured something that Madeline couldn't quite hear, although she thought, if she wasn't mistaken, she heard the word "escape." And then... there was no mistaking it — something about Maxfeld.

"What was that?" she asked, leaning over Drake, no longer considerate at all about politeness. She fixed Benjamin with her stare. "What did you say about Maxfeld?"

"Miss Castleton," Drake murmured in her ear, "it's nothing."

She turned her head to him quickly, shocked at just how close his face was to hers, but refusing to give in. This was too important.

"Pardon me?"

"I said—"

"I heard what you said." She fixed her glare on him. "But if this is about Kurt Maxfeld, then I deserve to know what has happened."

Benjamin looked over to Alice, who nodded at him, and Madeline was grateful that at least someone in this room was confident that she could handle whatever was to come.

"Madeline…" Benjamin said with some hesitation, "it seems that Kurt Maxfeld has escaped."

"Escaped?" Madeline exclaimed as her heart started thumping. "But… I thought he was in Newgate."

"He was," Benjamin said dryly. "But when they went to give him his supper tonight, he was gone. I only just received word of it before we sat down to dinner."

"Were you going to tell me?" Madeline asked, looking around the table at the shocked faces who all stared at her with expressions of dismay and pity. Horror covered Bennett's face.

"Of course," Benjamin said quietly, although from the way he looked away from her, she couldn't be entirely sure. At least she knew that Alice would have.

Drake placed a hand on the small of her back. No one else — except maybe Rose beside her — would be able to see the gesture, but a warming energy seemed to radiate from where he touched her, and she took a deep breath, letting it flow through her.

"Don't worry," he said, his voice a caress. "Maxfeld would have no need to come after you. You know nothing that could hurt him any further, and he doesn't need anything from you anymore."

Madeline took another deep breath. He was right. And yet…

"Madeline will need someone looking out for her all

hours of the day," Bennett said, rising from his place down the table. "There is too much at risk."

"She should be safe," Drake said, his words easy, measured, and Madeline appreciated his calm, steady sureness in such a situation as well as the fact he didn't falsely placate her. She supposed that was what made him the detective that he was.

"*Should* be?" Bennett's voice rose in pitch and volume, near to hysterics, and the contrast between the two of them was almost comical. "But what if she's not? Oh, what would her father think? I was supposed to be watching out for her, and now she is at the mercy of these men once again."

It took a moment for Bennett's words to invade Madeline's mind.

"Bennett... did you say that you were *supposed* to watch out for me?"

"Yes," he said, drawing himself up to his full height. "I told your father—"

Madeline pinched the bridge of her nose. It seemed that her father didn't trust her as much as she thought he did — not if he sent her cousin to oversee her. No wonder Bennett had recently taken a more active role in the business.

Suddenly it seemed as though everything was being launched at her like individual, relentless, pounding stones — the attack on the business, the frustrating inability to do anything about it, her convoluted feelings toward Drake, the fact her father didn't seem to actually trust her as she thought he did, and finally, the last stone hurtling toward her like a boulder rumbling down the hill, picking up speed as it went — Maxfeld's escape from prison.

She pushed back away from the table.

"Excuse me one moment, please."

And then, with all eyes staring after her, she did all she

could to keep her footsteps measured and even, holding her head high as she walked out of the dining room.

But the moment she turned the corner, meeting the corridor beyond, she couldn't hold back any longer.

She ran.

CHAPTER 11

Drake watched her leave the room, calmly, assuredly, but with a tension surrounding her that was palpable, a tightly wound control that she was doing her very best to hold onto, but that he could sense was slowly slipping away from her.

As conversation continued around the table, he and Alice shared a look, silently deciding who should go after Madeline. Drake was shocked by just how desperately he wanted it to be him. As Benjamin had been sharing the news of Maxfeld's escape with her, he had wanted nothing more than to reach his arms out and pull her in toward him, to tell her that everything was going to be all right — that he was there and would make sure that no harm would come to her.

But he couldn't. That wasn't his place. He was a detective on a case involving her business. If he was able to find Maxfeld, he would most certainly detain him and make sure he would never escape Newgate again, but as for comforting Madeline—

Before he or Alice could make any decision however,

Bennett was standing and following Madeline out the door and down the hall. Drake watched him go with narrowed eyes, which was ridiculous. This man was Madeline's family, and of course he should be there for her.

Alice shrugged at him with a small lift of her shoulders that told him it wasn't what she had wanted either, but there really wasn't anything either of them could do.

Drake sighed as the second course was placed in front of him. Any other time, the feast that was spread out before him on the elaborately decorated table would have been welcomed. Alice certainly had a flair for extravagance, but these people around the table made him feel far more comfortable than any who would typically accompany this involved meal.

"Everything all right?" Luxington asked from beside him, as though sensing the despair that had suddenly struck him, and Drake nodded and came back to himself.

"Yes, of course," Drake said, hoping this time he had done a more admirable job of masking his emotions. "I'm troubled about Maxfeld, but I do think he will leave Miss Castleton be. At least, I should hope he would. He has done enough."

Benjamin nodded slowly in agreement, but his brow was furrowed.

"Do you think he will, though? The truth is, we do not know much about him. He is not the man he presented himself to be, but an altogether different one. He could be out for revenge. I'm a bit worried myself, as he and Chesterpeak schemed so masterfully that it was difficult to see the truth. I'll certainly be keeping a close eye on Alice, that is for sure."

Drake moved some of the food around on his plate.

"I understand what you are saying. I'll speak to the other detectives. Perhaps there is more we can do to help keep Miss Castleton safe as well."

"Very good," Benjamin said. "Alice will be happy to hear it."

Drake nodded. He had an idea of just how he could ensure Madeline's safety. He would like to say that idea included him being there for her at all moments of the day, but he didn't have any particularly inspired ideas for devising a reason to remain close to her for that long a period of time. He would do his best — and he did know someone who could and not be questioned. He just had to convince her to agree to it.

Madeline and Bennett returned to the room while the course was being cleared away. Drake wasn't pleased with the fact that her face had seemingly lost all color, her expression reminding him of what she had looked like when he had first met her, after Maxfeld had nearly killed her. The protector in him wanted to wrap her up tightly in his arms, holding her so close that no harm could ever come to her.

When she retook her seat beside him, he couldn't help himself. Beneath the table, he reached over, wrapping his fingers around one of the hands that was balled tightly into a fist on her lap. She had removed her gloves for dinner, and her fingers were so icy cold that it nearly chilled him through just holding them. He squeezed her hand, as though he could impart reassurance and confidence that they would get through this just from his touch.

At first, she seemed to resist, her hands remaining in their fists, until suddenly she released them, her unyielding grip now encompassing his own hand, squeezing with a strength that he didn't know she had within her.

Drake held on tightly, willing to provide whatever she needed — in that moment, and for the foreseeable future. For the truth was, he had no desire to ever let go.

* * *

"I feel so foolish."

Madeline looked up at the understanding faces that surrounded her. The ladies had retired to the drawing room following dinner. They wouldn't remain alone long; the men said they would join them after one more drink.

"Why would you feel foolish?" Alice demanded.

"I've allowed him to affect me so greatly again. He escaped prison, yes, but what could he want to do with me anymore? I was a pawn in his game. I meant nothing besides a payout for him. He couldn't want anything to do with me again. Why would I even consider it?"

Her breaths were still shallow, uneven, but she had managed to gain enough control over her emotions that no one else was aware of her agitation.

"I think you are right," Alice agreed. "At least, I hope you are. But it would be wise to be careful until they find him again."

Madeline nodded. She wished she could have been stronger, could have remained there in the room with the rest of them and not run off like a child afraid of the dark. Bennett had been lovely and said all the right things when he had come after her, finding her in the parlor at the front of the house, but he had not been particularly reassuring — especially when he told her that he would keep her safe. Bennett was an agreeable sort, but he was not the man she would trust with her life.

Not like Drake.

One thing she could not share with the ladies was how reassuring his grip on her hand had been. His strength had flowed through her, filling her, comforting her. But to speak the words aloud would be to put too much of her own hope into them. For, despite their kiss, she refused to allow anyone in close again.

No matter how handsome or considerate he might be.

"Alice?" Benjamin was at the door. "We are going to play billiards, if that's all right?"

Alice nodded, but then looked around at the rest of them. "Shall we join in, ladies?"

Most men would likely have been surprised at the sentiment — but not Benjamin Luxington. He had been married to Alice for long enough to never be shocked at anything she might propose.

"Have you played before?" Rose asked Madeline as they followed Alice to the billiards room at the back of the house.

"Once or twice, when Alice thought it would be a bit of fun," Madeline said. "But I certainly don't expect to be anything near to proficient."

Rose nodded, biting her lip, and Madeline considered what this must all be like for her. The woman had barely spent any time away from Lyme, as far as Alice had told her, and here she was in a house full of strangers playing billiards of all things.

"We don't have to play," Madeline said, trying to provide her a way out. "I'm not entirely interested myself."

Rose drew her frame up to her full height, as though instilling confidence in herself. "I'm here," she said with a shrug and a small smile. "Might as well give it a go!"

Madeline nodded, wishing she could possess the same level of confidence as this woman, but unsure of just how to go about accomplishing that.

When they entered the room, however, instead of taking a seat near the wall as she would typically have done, Madeline surprised them all by taking a cue, agreeing to play.

Drake looked over at her, his eyes, typically hooded to shield his expression, widened somewhat, although she thought — or maybe she just hoped — that there was a bit of admiration in them.

"We have even numbers," Alice said, stepping up and

commanding the room, as she always did so well. "What do you say we pair up and have a bit of a game?"

She went around the room and told them who their match was — all husbands and wives, until she got to Rose. "Rose, you shall pair Mr. Castleton, and Madeline, you and Drake can be together."

Madeline nearly rolled her eyes at the twinkle within Alice's gaze, but Alice simply grinned at her impishly before joining her husband.

Their hosts first played Lord and Lady Exner, who they beat handily, before they had some trouble against Mr. and Mrs. Thompkins. Rose and Bennett were abysmal, although Bennett had much to say about the unfairness of the situation, since Alice and Benjamin obviously made full use of their billiards table.

"We do practice rather often," Alice said without a bit of shame. "Now, Madeline, Drake, let's see what you have."

Drake and Benjamin hit their cue balls, which traveled the length of the table, bounced off the cushion, and returned toward them. When they came to a stop, Drake's cue ball rested nearest the baulk cushion at the other end. He then chose to break, and quickly scored ten points before it was Alice's turn.

"Have you much experience?" Madeline asked him, but he shook his head. "Ah, so you are one of those men who is good at basically anything you attempt?" she asked with a rueful chuckle, but when he looked over to her, his expression was not one of mirth. Instead, Madeline was shocked to see that his stare had turned dark, with something else playing within his eyes and around the corners of his mouth.

"I am good at nearly everything I try, as long as I put some effort into it."

Madeline became very aware that he was no longer

speaking of billiards. Her mouth turned dry and she swallowed hard as her insides seemed to melt into liquid.

It was not as though she was some innocent woman — not anymore — but while the man she had known as Stephen, her husband, had been fun and amorous at first, he had never made her feel like this. When Madeline was close to Drake, when he kissed her, when he looked at her like he was right now, he created a longing the likes of which she had never before experienced.

And she wasn't sure whether or not she liked it.

She licked her lips and took a deep breath, as, after Alice sank the red ball, resulting in three points, she missed scoring, and it was Madeline's turn.

She missed. Missed completely.

"Damn it," she cursed, surprising even herself, and most especially Drake, who chuckled in her ear.

"Try again," Alice encouraged from across the table.

"No, it's fine," Madeline said, waving her hand, not wanting to suffer the embarrassment twice over. But with a little encouragement from around the table, she finally forced herself to step up once more.

"Here," Drake said, coming up behind her. "I'll help this time."

He was close, although not close enough to be *completely* improper. His arms came around her, one on each side, and he slid one warm hand down the cue to cover hers, bare from when she had removed the gloves as she began to play. Why was he always so hot and fiery?

"Now," he murmured, his mouth dangerously close to her ear, "back and forward, just like that."

She allowed him to guide the pool cue, and then when she struck the white ball and it went flying toward one of the red ones, sending it deep into a pocket, she cried out in elation.

She turned around to find Drake grinning down at her, and then he waved to the table.

"Your turn," he said. "Try again — on your own this time."

She couldn't deny that she missed the feeling of his arms around her, but she also took a deep breath to fill herself with confidence as she stepped up to the table. This time, she struck the white ball again, and while it simply glanced off another ball, it was still, to her, a victory.

She stepped back, hiding the small, proud smile that threatened to emerge, before Benjamin took his turn. He made one small mistake, and soon Drake was up again. The four of them continued, with Drake scoring most of their points, until they were tied, each only three away from three hundred.

And it was Madeline's turn.

"It's up to you," Drake said, when she turned to look at him imploringly for help. "You've got this."

She really didn't think she did, but there was nothing left to do but try.

She stepped up, closed one eye, and took aim.

And sank the red ball.

She stood there in shock for a moment, staring after it, then looking up to Drake.

"I did it," she said somewhat softly. "My goodness!"

"You did," he said, his lips beginning to curl.

Madeline just about jumped up and threw herself into his arms in celebration, but she held herself back at the last moment, remembering where they were. In a room full of people, one of them being her cousin, who she was sure would not approve and would most assuredly report back to her father.

Bennett began to clap, and her cheeks flushed when she saw that she was the center of attention once more — not somewhere she enjoyed finding herself.

"Thank you," she said softly, before slinking back into the shadows. When another game began, this time with the men only, she decided that she needed a bit of air — and she slipped out the door, unnoticed.

CHAPTER 12

Drake could tell that Madeline thought she had succeeded in surreptitiously leaving the room, but there was a truth that he was going to have to face — he would always notice her.

Not anymore.

When she had won the game for them, he had seen the elation on her face, knew how much it meant to her to have achieved what she had deemed impossible. And he was happy he had been the one to help her along.

It was inconsequential — a stupid billiards game — and yet, it contained more meaning than he wanted to admit.

He set his cue down and followed her out the door, catching a glimpse of her pink skirt retreating down the corridor before she entered the drawing room. He followed as she pushed through the sash window doors, stepping out into the small garden that backed the house, across the street from the mews.

She slipped her gloves back on as she took a seat on a bench, facing the dark alley beyond. There was little light out here, but the moon streamed down and the stars beyond her blanketed the sky and provided a backdrop that made her appear as though she was suspended in the air herself.

Drake ran a hand through his hair, wondering if he should go to her or not. There was something about this woman that called to him, that reached beyond the wall he had carefully erected and into his heart.

He had no wish for her there, but it didn't seem like his heart cared what his mind preferred anymore.

He paused once more in the doorway. He had a choice. He could turn around, return to the billiards room, and allow her some time alone. Or he could enter into the night and join her, putting himself at risk to be caught by the spell she didn't even know she was weaving.

His feet decided for him as he stepped out into the night.

* * *

MADELINE KNEW HE WAS THERE.

She had sensed him the moment he opened the garden doors behind her, knew he was standing there on the step, yet to enter into the night with her.

She closed her eyes as she waited. Waited for him to realize this was foolish, that he shouldn't be out here with her, that he should turn around and go back into the house with the others, to rejoin the billiards game and forget about her.

Then she heard his shoe scuff the dirt behind her, and her heart leaped even as her mind cried no.

"It's a beautiful night."

His words, soft and low, thrummed through her. He was so close, just a step away.

"It is," she said, her words breathy, her heart beginning to hammer in her chest.

She was aware now that this was more than just a conversation in which he would ensure that she was well. He was not out here to check on her. He was out here to meet with her, to greet her, to *be* with her.

Though in what sense, she was not entirely sure.

"You'll miss your turn," she noted, finally turning around to look up at him.

The moon reflected off the planes of his face, leaving his eyes dark and hidden from her, frustrating her with the inability to read his emotions.

"That's all right," he said with a small shrug. "They probably prefer that I do not return and take all of their money once more."

"If only our couples' game had been for money, we could have won ourselves a prize."

"What would you have done with it?" he asked, raising an eyebrow.

"I'm not sure. Maybe…"

"Yes?"

"Maybe I would have used it to go see the sculpting mastery of the ancient Greeks," she said, ducking her head. "I admire them. I've tried to review paintings, to copy their pre-eminence in my own work, but I can't quite seem to get it right."

"Your work?" he said, taking a seat beside her, and she shivered from where their thighs touched. "Do you mean with the stone?"

She nodded. "Most of our stone is used for statues and other edifices. I first became interested in the business when I would accompany my father to Castleton Stone and he would let me go into the factory and work with the clay to create sculptures of my own. It turned out that I had something of an aptitude for it."

Knowing her, she was being modest.

"Do you still sculpt?" he asked, and she shrugged.

"Now and then, when I find the time," she said.

"You should find the time," he insisted. "And you should see your statues."

"I will," she said with a nod. "One day."

He was silent for a moment, before he reached over and picked up one of her hands. He began to tug at the end of each of the fingers of her glove, until he slipped it right off. He turned her bare hand over within his, as if by examining it he could see just how she managed to sculpt.

"Your hands are beautiful," he said, to which she emitted a half-laugh, half-snort.

"My hands are plain. Ordinary."

"Nothing about you is ordinary."

"How can you say that, when you have likely met more interesting people than anyone else I have ever been acquainted with?"

"That is exactly why," he said. "I have met many people, you are right. And yet, you are the only one from whom I cannot keep away. Why is that?"

He had drawn closer to her, and now, finally, she could see into his eyes. They were dark and stormy, full of intrigue. She now wanted nothing more than to solve the mystery of this man, even though *he* was the investigator.

"About that, I have no idea," she said, biting her lip. "I suppose you will have to figure that out for yourself."

He dipped his head then, softly pressing his lips against hers, his question this time not in words, but by tasting, retreating, then returning again. She answered him by lifting her hands up around his neck and kissing him back with equal measure, her lips melding against his as though that was what they had been created for, to join with his and complete this puzzle of the two of them together.

With a primitive grunt he reached over, apparently not particularly pleased by the awkward position the bench placed them in, and lifted her so that she was sitting side-saddle on his lap. She was slightly taller than he now, and she couldn't help but enjoy the position it placed her in. She twined her fingers in his hair, the coarseness of it somehow also silky soft as it curled around her bare fingers.

Madeline shifted slightly and when he groaned, she suddenly became very aware of the rigid length of him beneath her bottom.

She smiled into his mouth and wiggled slightly, causing him to throw back his head with a supplication that echoed out into the night.

"God help me, Madeline, if you do that again I shall have to lay you back on this bench and take you right here."

She laughed in shock at his words, feeling the siren as she stroked the side of his face.

"What a promise," she said, this sultry side of her she never knew existed filling her with power that strengthened her with an indescribable headiness.

"Who *are* you?" he asked on a loud whisper as he took her lips once more, and the truth was, she had no idea. She was only just finding that out for herself, but she had to admit, she kind of liked this woman she was discovering, this woman who had been hiding for so long, between all that was expected of her and all that she had thought to be true.

At one point in time she had supposed that she needed a man, especially a man who could better her in society, to make her life worthwhile. When she had been disillusioned about that, she had determined that she needed the business to sustain her worthiness. Now, while she still desperately longed to prove that Castleton Stone could be hers, she was beginning to realize that the business did not define who she was. It was part of her, but it wasn't her.

She was a woman in and of herself. A woman she could be proud of.

A woman who deserved this interlude in the garden with a man who went by the name of Drake and Drake alone.

It might be a moment of fantasy, but it was one she would take.

His tongue tangled with hers, and she matched his intensity with a ferocity she didn't know she had within her. He ran his hands up and down her sides, as though with a bit of force and touch he could magically make her dress disappear, and, for a moment, with the mystique of the night around them, she wondered if he, in fact, could do so. He seemed to be capable of everything else.

He shifted her now so that she was straddling him, and as he cupped her bottom so that she could feel every glorious inch of him, she wondered just what it would be like to have him deep within her. While the night wasn't quite magical enough to make her believe it was possible out here in the gardens with but one brick wall between them and the rest of the party, she knew that, perhaps, it *could* happen at some point, if she would allow it. If he would allow it. If they could both overcome everything that was holding them back and find the promise that could bring them together.

"You're amazing," he murmured as he cupped her breast, her nipple hardening through the fabric of her dress, her shift, and her stays, which he began to find his way below to really feel her, and she arched up into him.

"Mmm," was all she could manage as she pushed into his hand, suddenly wishing they were somewhere else, somewhere they could take full advantage of one another. Her breaths came hard and fast, and when his mouth rejoined hers, this time there was nothing soft and sweet about his kiss. He ravaged her with his lips, his tongue, and she wondered about the stark desperation there, until she could wonder no more as her thoughts fled and she acted only on instinct and emotion, matching him with a rawness, a vulnerability that she had never wanted to expose, that she had never done so, even to the man she had thought was her husband.

But Drake… he was something else. He was someone else. Someone she never wanted to let go of.

However, everything must come to an end, she realized as he came to his senses first, pulling back away from her. She had no idea how long they had been outside, away from the party. Had they been missed? Likely, but she found she didn't overly care.

She wondered how he could have been of enough mind to stop, but he hadn't forgotten what she needed as he reached out and, with surprisingly gentleness, began to restore her to rights. He tucked a strand of hair behind her ear, his touch there nearly as erotic as on her breast. He lifted her bodice to ensure that it covered her appropriately, and, finally, set her down in front of him, back on her feet.

"There," he said, looking her over from head to toe. "You look the proper woman once again. Not thoroughly ravished."

She met his eye. For she was not as thoroughly ravished as she would like to be. Not even close. "Do you think anyone will guess what we have been up to?"

He gave a low laugh, a laugh filled with promise. "I absolutely do. And I don't care one bit."

Her eyes widened at that. "But they will all think—"

"Madeline." He stopped her. "Why do you care so much what they think, or what anyone thinks at that? The only thing that you need to worry about is that customers know that you are trustworthy, and suppliers know that you are loyal. That is what your business is based upon, is it not?"

"It is," she said softly.

"Well, then. Those people in there are your friends. This is what Mrs. Luxington wanted, anyway, is it not?"

She laughed at that, although in a rueful way, as though she never should have given in to what her friend wanted so badly. "It most certainly is."

"Well, then, the worst of it is that you proved her right and you shall never hear the end of this."

Madeline sighed. "Of that, you can be certain."

CHAPTER 13

They were right.

Alice was in all of her glory.

The moment Madeline and Drake had returned to the billiards room with the rest of them last night, Alice had been watching her with a wide, smug, knowing smile on her face. Madeline had rolled her eyes at her and waved her away, but Alice hadn't stopped her persistence until Madeline finally relented and shared a very small bit of what had occurred outside.

Alice had nearly crowed her triumph.

It had been the last Madeline had spoken to Drake that evening, however. Before she could ask him about meeting with Powers the next day, he was gone, leaving the dinner so abruptly that half of them hadn't even known he had left.

Now, this morning, she had to hope that he would inform her of when and where he was going. Her wish was that if that kiss — well that kiss and more, much more — meant anything, it was that he trusted her now, and would no longer suspect that she had anything to do with Castleton Stone's problems.

She stepped onto the cobblestones outside of her factory, looking up at the three-story golden brick building with some pride — this could be hers one day, with her father trusting her with it even today, while he was away.

It was early, the hour when very few would be within the building, but the dawn light breaking over the thatched roof meant that some of her sculptors would be here, those who found their creativity peaked in the early hours.

It was when she herself found that her fingers worked best.

"Good morning, Thomas," she greeted one of their oldest employees, who was sitting near the window, allowing the light to shine on the clay he was beginning to form into a gargoyle mold, which would create many statues that would most assuredly spend their lives sitting high up on a turret, inspecting all before them.

"Good morning, Miss Castleton," he replied, taking a quick break to look up at her. "'Tis good to see you. Been some time."

"It has," she agreed. "Far too long."

She laid out her tools on the worktable next to him, donning an apron overtop of her dress.

"Anything in particular that needs to be done today?" she asked.

"A pair — but not an identical one — to what I'm working on," he said, "but I'll do that myself later. There's a lion that's just come out of the kiln that needs a firm hand to bring it to life. We're to incorporate the family crest along with it."

"Oh!" she exclaimed. "How intriguing. I would love to take it on."

He gave her the size requirements and she began to sculpt, as slowly and surely as she could, perfecting the lion into the life-like beast it was to become.

As always happened, she became so involved in her task

that she forgot everything else around her — the business' problems, her father's potential scandal, and, of course, Drake.

Well, if she was being honest, she did not entirely forget Drake. One could never wholly forget him.

She just allowed him to fall to the side for a moment as her task took over, and she wished, for a moment, that everything else could come as simply and as naturally as this.

"Miss Castleton?"

Madeline looked up with a start, unsure of what time it was, or how long she had been focused. The lion was already looking quite ferocious, however, with the family crest emerging, so she had to guess that it had been a couple of hours, at the very least.

"Yes, Thomas?"

"While you were working, a missive came in. It was delivered to me, as I oversee the sculptors, but it should go to you."

"Oh?" she said, reaching out a hand to take the letter from him, holding open the crinkled page.

Her heart sank as she read it. It seemed that Sawyer Jackson, one of her finest sculptors, was leaving Castleton Stone — for Treacle.

"Oh, no," she said, looking up at Thomas beseechingly. "Jackson has been with us nearly as long as you have, Thomas. I don't understand it."

Thomas ran a hand over his short hair as he shifted from one foot to the other.

"I—I cannot say, Miss."

She sighed and stood, abandoning the lion — for now. She would come back to it later that evening, when all of the work was finished.

She laughed to herself silently. Who was she kidding? The work was never finished.

As she looked around the factory — the premises her father had worked so hard to build — the growing despair in her belly began to take on an edge. An edge of anger.

Who did Jeremiah Treacle think he was, that he could poach her artists, her stone, her business? He may have made others believe that he was innocent of any wrongdoing, but she knew better. He had to be behind this.

"Madeline?" Bennett walked into the warehouse, as immaculately dressed as ever. "What's the matter?"

"Treacle is now stealing our people, not just our product," she said, her hands on her hips.

"They what? What do you mean?"

"They have hired Jackson away from us. It's not right. Not at all. I am going to Treacle. They have to understand that they cannot take what is mine."

"That's all well and good, Miss Castleton," Thomas said, his hands now clasped behind him as he rocked back and forward on his heels uncomfortably, "but before you do…"

"Yes?"

"Well, it's just that, there might be another reason why Jackson left."

"Oh?" She could hardly imagine why. Castleton Stone employees were treated better than nearly any others she knew.

"We didn't receive our pay last week," Thomas said, scuffing a toe into the floor.

Madeline furrowed her brow.

"You must be mistaken, Thomas," she said, "for I approved it myself."

"We never received it," Thomas mumbled.

"But… I don't see how that is even possible!" Madeline exclaimed, throwing her hands in the air. "Even if it was so, why would no one tell me?"

"Well…" Thomas shrugged. "We thought, perhaps, with

all of the difficulties the business has been having, and what with your father being gone, we should just wait until Castleton Stone returned to its usual prominence."

"Or do you mean perhaps..." Madeline said with a lifted eyebrow, "wait until my father returns?"

"Yes," Thomas said, looking down, unable to meet her eye, and Madeline took a breath as she tried to keep from any sort of exclamation. It was not Thomas' fault. Not in the slightest.

She turned to regard her cousin. "Bennett," she said firmly, "did you not pay all of our workers?"

He looked at her somewhat guiltily. "I do not recall you approving the payments to go out."

"Bennett," she said with exasperation, "I signed everything off myself, then provided it to you. All you had to do was to actually give it to the employees. Did you or did you not do so?"

"I'm so sorry, Madeline," he said, looking up at her with supplication, his hands out, palms up, in front of him. "I sincerely didn't see them. They were not on your desk. And the truth is, I thought the same as Thomas."

"Where could they possibly have gone?"

"Perhaps the same person who stole the product stole the payments."

"But why?" she said, having to keep from practically wailing the question. She had to keep hold of any pride she possibly had left.

"I don't know, Madeline, and I'm so sorry," Bennett said, his voice softening. "But perhaps... perhaps it is time to ask your father to come home. Immediately."

"And admit my defeat?" she said defiantly, but Bennett shrugged.

"I understand that you want to prove yourself, Madeline,

truly I do," he said. "And I am well aware that without all of the setbacks, you would have prospered. You are made for this business. But. Sometimes things happen that are beyond our control. As hard as this is to say, I implore you to not allow your pride to come first, over what is best for the business."

Madeline took a deep breath as she began to pace back and forth across the earth-packed factory floor, her hands on her hips. She knew Bennett was trying to be helpful, but what could her father do that would be any different from what she would do? The only thing that might change is whoever was after her might stop.

"I'll think about it," she said, and when Bennett began to protest, she held up a hand. "I said I would think about it," was all that she promised, and then she continued. "First, we need to make sure that everyone gets paid."

"Very well, I will—"

"No," she shook her head. "I shall do it myself."

She realized she was still wearing the smock, and she lifted it over her head as she made for the stairs to where the offices were located.

"I shall be back, Thomas, you can promise the workers that," she said. She placed a foot on the stair and a hand on the railing, when she suddenly felt that she was being watched. She looked up to find Drake standing at the top of the stairs, leaning on the railing as she ascended.

"How long have you been here?" she asked as he watched her without expression, and she wished more than ever that he was freer with his emotions. Had last night meant anything at all to him? Was he here because he *wished* to be here, or because she was paying him to be here? And had he witnessed another of her failings?

"Long enough," he answered her. "You've been targeted again."

"I have," she said with a sigh. "But what I just don't understand is how it happened."

She reached him and continued on past him, but held the door open for him to follow. He accepted her invitation to join her and they walked toward her office at the back of the corridor. When they reached it, however, she didn't sit down, but instead, walked over to the window, looking out at the view it offered of the Thames beyond.

"What am I doing wrong?" she murmured. "Why can I not find my way through this?"

"I must apologize," Drake said, surprising her with both the sentiment as well as his proximity, just over her shoulder. "I have not been as helpful as I should be. I have been preoccupied."

"With another case?" she asked, turning to look at him.

"No, not entirely," he shook his head, his eyes hooded. "Something else. Something personal."

"Is it… anything I can help with?" she asked, wanting to know more, but it was yet one more thing he did not seem to deem her important enough to share.

"No," he shook his head. "I must take care of it myself."

At his inability to trust her and her own inability to encourage him to open up, she lost all fight that was within her.

"Perhaps Bennett is right," she said, turning around and leaning her head back against the window. "Perhaps I should just give up and write my father to ask him to come home."

Drake studied her, his dark eyes roving over her face, as though he could find every answer he ever sought within.

"Is that what you want?"

She stared back at him, wishing he would tell her what to do, that he could solve it all and make all of her problems disappear.

"I—"

"This is your business — at least for the moment, Madeline," he said, using her given name for the first time, and it warmed her right through, telling her, that, perhaps, he did feel something more for her than this arrangement. "This is your life, and your decision. No one can make it for you. Not me, not your cousin, not your father. You."

His words struck something deep within her, a chord that vibrated through every bone and muscle of her being.

He was right. This was her decision. This was her company, and no one else could make the decision for her.

People had been deciding things for her for far too long. She had taken a chance before, and it had been the wrong one, yes. But Kurt Maxfeld could not steal her life away unless she let him.

"I want to fight this myself," she said, the words coming out before she had even realized she had made the decision. "I want to determine who is trying to use me and what they see as my weakness to bring down this company, and I want to take them on." She looked him squarely in the eye. "Will you help me?"

He grinned then, finally showing her something — that he approved of her answer. Not that it mattered. She knew what she had to do.

"Absolutely," he said, and then leaned in, brought one of his large hands to the back of her head, and kissed her.

She gripped the lapels of his jacket, holding him to her greedily. She didn't need this, she didn't need him — she was fine on her own — but she could not deny how liberating it was to choose this, to allow this joy that he brought her to course through her veins, bringing to life a side of her that she had thought would never return.

Even if this was only a moment in time, she would take it, and be happy, be joyful, be proud of who she was and what she was doing — including the choice to be with him, in whatever way was possible.

He leaned back, the grin gone, but satisfaction toying with the sides of his lips. "Now tell me, Miss Castleton—" so they were back to that again, "—would you like to accompany me on an interview with Mr. Hubert Powers?"

She smiled up at him, his invitation more empowering and telling than anything he could ever say to her. "Why yes, Drake. Yes, I would."

CHAPTER 14

Drake couldn't have said when he decided to include Madeline in the rest of his investigation.

Maybe it was when he had first arrived and had watched her bent over the sculpture she was working on. The lion had appeared, slowly and beautifully, until he realized that it was not a lion but a lioness that was emerging from the clay.

A lioness that reminded him of her.

Maybe it was when she had heard the news that she had, yet again, been sabotaged. She had taken it stoically, but he could tell how much it had broken her — especially the fact that loyalty to her had been questioned.

Or maybe it had been when everyone else — her cousin included — seemed to be questioning her competence. He understood it. She was a woman, one who did not seem particularly strong on the surface, trying to prove herself in a world where she would never be entirely accepted.

And so he decided to give her this one opportunity — and let her do with it what she would.

He had never been so proud as when she took it.

So much so, he had kissed her before even realizing just what he was doing.

And he had started wondering... if perhaps he had been wrong. Wrong about closing himself off to all opportunities for love or connection with another person — most especially a woman. For when he was with Madeline, everything just seemed... different somehow. Better. Brighter. Brimming with possibilities he never would have imagined before.

But what would it mean to be with her? After everything she had gone through, she deserved a man who could give her the life that she had dreamed of, a life of extravagance, who could be her partner in every way.

He was never home. He had no time or inclination to provide for a woman or for a family. They only spent so much time together now because she currently *was* his work.

He could, however, brighten her life while he had this time with her. Which he would do today — after the work finished.

He waited for her outside of her factory, as she emerged through the doors and down the rather rickety stairs with a reticule in her hand and a bonnet on her head. He stared up at her once she came into view, taking a moment just to appreciate the pretty picture she made with the Thames in the background, the red brick of her factory door surrounding her.

Tendrils of her blond hair brushed the side of her face, sweeping away in the wind. She reminded him of the statue of a siren, meeting the waves of a ship. The Queen of the Thames. He placed his hand in his pockets, rocking back and forth on his heels as he took a moment to appreciate her gentle beauty.

And realized that this was something he never did. He never stopped to consider anything around him.

He would stop and think, but it was always to review a case or consider notes he had made, to puzzle together random clues that otherwise didn't make any sense.

Aesthetics meant nothing to him — while it was her world.

She looked from one side to the other, until finally she spotted him and stopped, her blue eyes fixing on him. She lifted a hand somewhat tentatively and waved, which spurred him into action once more as he climbed a couple of steps until he was close enough to reach out to her.

"Miss Castleton," he greeted her with a nod, and she lifted an eyebrow at him, smiling in a shyly seductive manner, as though she was attempting to tease him but unsure entirely how to go about doing so.

"No 'Madeline' anymore?" she asked, her lids dropping to shutter her gaze, and he reached out his other hand, using the back of his index finger to lift her chin so that she was looking at him again.

"Madeline, then, if I have permission to call you such."

"You do," she said, her blue eyes flashing with what seemed akin to hope.

"I am a fortunate man," he said before holding out an elbow to her. "Shall we?"

She looked up at him in surprise, which he understood. Aside from the instances in which desire took over all reason, they had treated one another in a purely professional manner. This almost suggested they were courting one another, or, at the very least, enjoying each other's company as any lady and gentleman would do.

When she laced her fingers over his forearm, he tucked it in close to his side, trying to remember the last time — or any time — he had ever escorted a woman this way.

And came up empty.

"Powers' warehouse isn't far," she said. "In fact, I have

never actually met him before. He has only ever dealt with my father. I was thinking we could pretend that I am your associate. That way he would have no reason to think that I have any motive in dealing with him."

"Why Miss Cas— Madeline, with all of your grand schemes, I am beginning to think that perhaps you could make a fine detective."

"I'm sure I would," she said with a small smile, "except that I am far too busy running a stone company."

He laughed at that, noticing as they walked that they — well, she — was drawing many admiring glances from men they passed.

"Here it is," she said, pointing to the grey building before them. "Not far at all. His building is adjacent to the docks, where many of the supplies are unloaded from incoming ships. The Thames is getting busier, however, and he'd like to expand. He has successfully bought the building next to ours, but wishes for ours as well."

"Your father has no thought to sell?"

She shook her head. "It's the ideal location for us. From enticing workers to come to us, to our water requirements, to shipping our own product to where it needs to go. To move would require not only a great investment in terms of relocating and reinstalling all of our equipment, but we would then have additional costs to transport all of our supplies as well as our finished product. It's just not worth it."

"And Powers is not exactly pleased with your refusal?"

"He is not." She shook her head. "I find it hard to believe he would resort to such methods as thievery and vandalism, but who is to say for sure?"

"People are capable of anything if they are sufficiently motivated," Drake said, his voice reflecting a dark tone, and she looked up at him sharply.

"What happened?" she asked.

He shook his head, not pretending he wasn't aware of what she spoke. "A story for another day," was all he said.

She stopped suddenly, so much so that her arm was nearly ripped from his grasp. "No," she said, and he looked back at her with some surprise.

"What's that?"

"I said no," she repeated, her jaw set firmly. "I would like to know what happened. And I would like you to tell me about it — at least some of it — now."

He stared at her as he breathed in, determined not to let her see just how much he didn't want to speak of it. "My parents were murdered."

* * *

DRAKE TURNED and began walking up to the building, leaving her with that bit of information and no explanation whatsoever.

Madeline gaped after him, her stomach churning at the news.

"Murdered?" she said, her voice just about a whisper. "But how — how do you know for sure? What happened? Do you know who? Do you—"

"Madeline," he said with patience yet also a hint of warning, "I will answer your questions later. I promise. But now is not the time. I cannot be thinking of that while I am here, trying to solve this, with you. Do you understand?"

She stood rigidly, suddenly feeling very much the chastised child. Her case was nothing. Inconsequential. People were killed. People were maimed. People were treated in all kinds of horrible ways. This... this was nothing. An inconvenience. No wonder he hadn't been particularly interested in helping her.

She swallowed her pride as she followed him to the door, now quite embarrassed about it all.

He held it open for her, his face belying none of what he truly felt for her question or for what they were doing there.

"We are here to see Mr. Powers," he told the clerk who greeted them. He nodded, nothing suspicious about his stare as he bid them to follow him through the brick-walled rooms, full of a wide assortment of various goods. Madeline stared at it all with interest, until she stopped rather suddenly, surprised to find, sitting in the corner, surrounded by all around him like Midas and his gold, a rather circular man. His head was a round egg, void of any hair, but complemented by an extravagant mustache that curled around the corners nearly up to his nose.

"Hello there," he greeted them. "How can I help the two of you today?"

Madeline allowed Drake to step forward and take charge of the conversation.

"I am Mr. Johnson, and this is my wife, Mrs. Johnson," he said, and Madeline was so shocked by his flat tone, his usual gravelly baritone, that she only realized belatedly he had referred to her as his wife.

She rather liked the sound of it.

Then she told herself not to be so stupid.

"We are here because we are interested in negotiating a contract with a shipping agent," he said. "We heard you were the man to speak to."

"You heard right," Powers said, his countenance changing to one much warmer and welcoming. "I am the finest in all of London. What sort of goods do you ship?"

"Fur," Drake said, and Madeline was both impressed and incredulous at how easily the lies slipped off his tongue as he committed to this role.

"Ah!" Powers' eyes lit up. "How interesting."

"I do have a concern however," Drake said, bringing his finger beside his mouth and nose as he actually appeared to be considering his dilemma. "Are you a large enough operation for my business? It seems that you do not have much space for ships to dock, and I hear you are already a very busy man."

"I am," Powers said confidently, pulling at the lapels of his jacket. "And I am busy because I am the very best. But not to worry — I shall be expanding soon."

"But how so, when you are surrounded? That is one thing we do not have to worry about over in America — if anything is plentiful, it is land."

"I can imagine," Powers said. "But as it happens, I will be taking over two of the neighboring businesses."

"Which ones?"

"The adjacent one," he said, pointing to the building next door, "and the one beyond that."

"Is that not a stone factory?" Madeline said, unable to keep herself from speaking. "I thought I saw some sculptures outside as we walked by."

"It is, Mrs. Johnson," he said, his tone changing to one that made it sound as though he was speaking to a child who required a great deal of explanation. "However, I have heard that they might be looking to sell soon. The owner has left it in the hands of his daughter. Can you imagine that?"

As he threw back his head and laughed, Madeline had to keep her jaw clenched tightly in order to fake the smile that Powers was expecting. Inside, however, she was fuming.

Drake placed his hand over hers, as though holding her back from saying anything further. She was about to tell him just exactly what she thought of *that* when he spoke.

"Perhaps, Mr. Powers, she is one exemplary female. Their product looks quite fine, indeed."

Powers shrugged. "I've heard they've had some setbacks.

Although if they don't sell, I can buy the building on the other side. It's not quite as desirable land, but it will do. Now, what do you say we draw up some contracts?"

Drake made excuses, promising to return later that day after he met with a few other agents.

As soon as they were out of earshot, Madeline was already shaking her head with a sigh. "I don't think he did it."

"No?"

"No," she said. "He wants the land, yes, but enough to go through additional effort to do so? I don't think so. Not if he has another option available to him."

"As it happens, I agree with you," Drake said with a nod.

"So who do you think it was?"

"I have some ideas," he said cryptically. "But first, there is somewhere I want to take you."

"Oh?"

"Something not related to this case. Or any case — at least any case of mine."

"Very well," she said, eyeing him as he held out his elbow once more.

"It's a bit of a walk, unless you'd fancy hiring a hack?"

"I think," she said, eyeing him with renewed determination, "that a lengthy walk sounds like the perfect time to continue our conversation."

CHAPTER 15

*D*rake had hoped with his harsh, surprising words earlier about his parents' untimely death that Madeline would have been scared away from asking anything further regarding the matter.

It seemed he was wrong. She was more tenacious than he had given her credit for.

She looked down and her voice softened. "I'm so sorry, Drake," she said. "I can't even imagine what that must have been like for you."

He nodded but said nothing, willing his jaw to stay firm.

"What happened?" she asked quietly but firmly.

It seemed she wasn't going to leave this be. He sighed, looking down at the paving stones at his feet, beside them at the red-brick buildings they passed, nodded to the fellow selling his wares at the side of the road. Anywhere but at Madeline.

"That's the thing," he finally said, realizing as he did so that this was the first time he had ever actually talked to anyone about it. "I'm not entirely sure. They went out one night, leaving me with my aunt and uncle. The situation became permanent, for they never came home."

"Where were they?"

"Apparently they were at some sort of gathering among friends," he said, "but no one was ever clear on where they were or what they were doing. My aunt and uncle refuse to speak to me of it any further."

"How old were you?"

"Eight."

"Oh, Drake," she said, and her words, so gentle and sympathetic, yet without the pity that accompanied most when they heard the story, tugged at him deep within, evoking emotions that had been lying dormant for so long he hardly even knew they existed anymore. "Will they speak of it now that you are not only an adult, but a detective?"

"No," he said, the word harsher than he had intended. "And that's the thing — I don't understand why. It's as if they are hiding something, although what there would be to hide, I have no idea."

"So this is why you joined Bow Street — in order to determine what happened?"

"Partially." He shrugged as he led her around a horse and cart that were standing still in the middle of the road. "It's been so long now, though, I don't know how I could ever possibly determine the truth. More so it spurred me to want to find justice for others — for those cases that I *could* solve."

"Mine must seem so minute to you," she said, bowing her head once more, and he realized that in his attempt to diminish the importance of his own situation, he must have made her feel that hers was of no consequence.

"I have every intention of solving your case."

"I know," she said, "and I do appreciate it."

"As for my parents' case... I did let it go. Or, at least, I had.

But I am now aware that there is someone who knows something. And that someone wants me to know as well."

She looked over at him sharply as he steered her around a cart that had been left at the side of the road, and he wondered just what had caused him to say such a thing. He had intended to keep the information to himself, for he knew that everyone else would tell him it was madness to even consider he could solve a case so many years later. Why he had said anything to her, he had no idea.

Yet somehow... he had a feeling that she would understand.

He was right.

"Did someone say something to you?" she asked, her gaze inquisitive.

"Something was sent to me," he said. "A satchel, with a pendant within."

She seemed intrigued. "A pendant? What kind of pendant?"

"To me it looks like a hawk, but I'm not actually sure of its purpose," he said.

She frowned, tapping a finger against her mouth and he was mesmerized for a moment by the motion, wishing he could feel the silky softness of those lips once more.

"That sounds familiar," she said, startling him out of his revelry.

"That's what everyone says."

"Can I see it?"

"I shall bring it to you," he promised, surprising himself. "Perhaps you might recognize it."

He doubted it, but it was worth trying. Anything was.

"And that is all?"

"That is all," he said. "Except that the satchel... it was my father's."

"Oh," she said, her mouth rounding and her brows lifting, "so whoever had it knows what happened to him."

He nodded grimly. "I believe so."

"Why send it to you? Why not just come tell you what happened?"

He let out a long exhalation as they rounded the corner. "That is part of what I am trying to determine."

He looked over at her with a sideways glance. "What do you think, then?" he asked, trying to keep his words nonchalant. "Do you think I should pursue it?"

She stopped altogether, causing a man walking behind them to curse at them when he had to swerve around them.

"How could you not?" she exclaimed, her features more animated than he had ever seen them. "Why, if it was my father, I would stop at nothing to determine what happened to him."

A sense of relief flooded through him. Relief that he was not mad for doing so, that *someone* believed in him — and that that someone was Madeline.

She looked over his shoulder suddenly. "We are at the museum."

"We are."

"What are we doing here?"

"Well," he said with a shrug, "I heard you say that you wanted to see the Greek masters. This may not be Greece but it is their work."

"The Elgin Marbles," she breathed.

"Have you ever seen them?" he asked.

She shook her head.

"A woman with your talent should have the opportunity to view work from the masters… although I cannot see how you would have anything to learn."

"What do you mean?"

"Only that your work is extraordinary."

"Oh," she said, her cheeks flooding with pink in a most becoming way. "I don't know about that."

"It's true," he said. "I—" Why he was admitting this, he had no idea. "I was watching you work. I could hardly believe how you made that lion come to life. You must be most sought after as a sculptor."

She laughed, lowly and wryly. "Hardly. No one wants work completed by a woman. Don't you know true artists are all men?"

"They wouldn't think that if they knew what you could do."

She shrugged. "It seems to be preferable to most that I keep the books and assist my father. Anything else is unforgiveable."

"Then make them see what they are missing by believing so," he said as he led her up the wide walkway and through the Doric columns.

She was silent once they entered, her curious gaze taking in all that surrounded them, and Drake wondered anew at what went on behind those wide blue eyes. She was an enigma, this woman. He was aware that most would assume the slightest adversity would break her, but she continued to prove how wrong it would be to presume such a thing. Most women would never have survived what she went through, yet here she was, not only standing, but rising. With the face of an angel, she was using her fiery sword to bring down any demon who flew into her path.

If he could help her in any way, he could. He *would*.

But first, today was for her — a bit of enjoyment in a world typically so void of it.

Following the directions from one of the staff members, they turned the corner into a large room, filled with works of art from Athens. But it was not the ancient Grecian sculptures that filled his gaze and stole his breath — no, it was the face of the woman beside him who captivated him. Her eyes were open wide as she took in all before her, her mouth a round O.

"Oh, Drake," she said, hugging his arm into her side. He was aware she likely didn't even realize what she was doing, but he enjoyed it all the same. "They are magnificent."

He looked at the sculptures through her eyes, watching her stare at them with such awe, and suddenly he wished he was one of those marble busts, headless or not.

She walked over to one — this one with head intact, although it was lacking both its hands and feet. The sculpted — both in plaster and in physique — form of the man nearly made him jealous, so reverently did she regard it.

She removed her glove, reaching out a hand and lightly running her fingertips over the muscled bicep. Now he really did wish he could switch places with the ancient Greek.

"The Parthenon Sculptures," she said quietly, and he wondered if she was talking to him or reviewing them for herself. "It's hard to believe they are here, in London."

"They have been for some time, have they not?"

"Yes," she said with a nod. "They were at Burlington House until a few years ago."

"Why have you not yet seen them?" he asked.

She tilted her head, still not looking directly at him. "I'm not sure. I suppose I was just too busy. I always thought I would go see them the next week or the next month, and then it just got to the point where there was always something else to do."

Drake rocked back and forth on his heels, his hands clasped behind him. "I can understand that."

"Have you ever seen them before?" she asked, finally looking at him, and he shook his head.

"No," he said. "I never had any wish to see them before. It

seemed a... frivolous activity for me. But you — you appreciate such things."

"Do you know their history?" she asked, and he wondered at the fact she never wanted to speak about herself.

"I am aware they are from Greece," he said, "and that Lord Elgin brought them to England."

"He did," she said, retracting her hand, re-covering it with her glove, and he mourned that loss of glimpse of skin. "They are from the Athenian Acropolis and were sculpted sometime around 440 BC. Much of the temple was destroyed during a war between Venice and the Ottomans."

"And now nothing remains."

She shrugged. "Lord Elgin claimed that Greece was destroying it all anyway, melting the stone down for lime. Who can know for sure? Anyway, this is said to be half of the originals. Parts of the frieze, the metopes, and figures from the pediments, among sculptures taken from elsewhere on the Acropolis."

"These are made of marble?"

"They are," she nodded. "Sometimes I wonder... our Castleton stone, it's beautiful, fine stone, and yet it is not as true in its form as these. Will our stone last two thousand years? Who is to know for sure? Will my sculptures remain in a museum someday, for others to gaze upon, wondering what I was thinking, why I created what I did? Likely not."

Her smile was sad, and he reached out a hand, lightly bringing it to her waist.

"I'm sorry. I did not bring you here to upset you."

"Oh, you didn't," she said, turning to him, the sides of her lips curving back up. "I am happy you brought me here. Seeing these... they have inspired me. My fingers are itching to return to my own creations, and not just those a client has commissioned to impress onlookers. It's also encouraged me to try my new formula, one that would allow me to truly sculpt."

"Would you like to look around first?"

"I would," she said, and she began to circle the room, which made him feel as though he was back in ancient Greece, with all of the gods and goddesses looking down upon him, watching his every move. Would he receive their approval, he wondered, or their ire?

He followed Madeline with his eyes, noting her study of each frieze and sculpture, how drawn in she was to them. He was never one to consider what men or women were capable of — it didn't much matter to him.

But watching her, noting her intelligence, listening to her ideas, hearing her speak, seeing the way she truly studied everything that came into her attention, he knew he would never doubt the capability of a woman again.

He stood as still as one of the statues until she returned to him, her reticule held tight in her hands and a dreamy smile on her face.

"I'm ready to go," she said, and he nodded and offered his arm.

"Thank you for bringing me here," she said as they exited the museum, although not before she pointed out the skeleton of the strange creature that Miss Ellis had discovered in Lyme Regis. Drake, however, was not one for the mythical, magical, or even historical creature. He had history enough to uncover without being concerned with giant beasts that would only haunt his nightmares.

"It was my pleasure," he said, turning to look at her, capturing her eyes in his, this time not allowing her to tear them away. "I enjoyed seeing you happy today."

She laughed lightly, self-consciously.

"I don't often take time to do anything for fun. Unless Alice forces me to."

"Well, today, I am the one doing so."

They talked about everything and nothing as they returned to Castleton Stone, and Drake couldn't remember the last time he had taken a moment to simply enjoy himself without purpose or expectation.

"Thank you, Drake," she said, and their steps seemed to slow as they approached the busy factory. "What comes next?"

"Next?" he said, his head jerking up in surprise. He couldn't deny that he had considered whether there actually *was* any place for her in his life, but—

"After interviewing Powers, what is your idea? What do we follow up on? And with the mystery surrounding your parents, we must—"

"Not to worry, Madeline," he said, cutting her off. There was no chance he was going to place Madeline in any sort of danger that might come with being involved in any of his investigations. "I will take care of it."

"But—"

"I promise," he said, "and I promise that I will come to you for any help I might need — with either case."

"Please do," she said softly, before silence reigned. There was so much he wanted to say, and yet he didn't know how — for putting it out there into the world seemed impossible, and he never wanted to make a promise he couldn't keep.

"Madeline," he said as they arrived at her factory, "there is something else."

"Oh?" She looked up at him expectantly.

"I cannot always be here to watch out for you, in part because it would not be entirely proper for me to do so."

"Of course not," she said softly, not meeting his gaze.

"So in the meantime, I am going to send one of my colleagues to do so."

"A colleague?"

"Yes," he said with a nod. "Miss Georgina Jenkins. She can pose as one of your friends, and it will not seem strange if she accompanies you anywhere you wish to go."

"A woman?" Madeline asked, raising her eyebrows.

"She is…" Drake looked around to ensure that no one was within earshot. "She is one of Bow Street's best-kept secrets. She is a detective, but most believe her to be not much more than a secretary. When necessary, however, she can be deadly with a weapon and is one of the most intelligent people I have ever met. You can rely on her for anything you might need."

Madeline nodded, although she still wouldn't meet his eye and her body had become rigid enough that he wondered just what he had said that would cause such a reaction.

"I can understand your reluctance, but I just want to keep you safe."

"Of course," she said, although her smile was forced. "I understand."

Unsure of what else to say, he gave her a nod. "Until the next time, Miss Castleton. Sculpt something for me, will you?"

"Perhaps," she said with a small twist of her lips, and then she was gone, inside the building.

And he wondered at the ache in his chest that followed after her.

CHAPTER 16

Madeline stood with some trepidation when the knock sounded on her office door. So here she was. The woman who would apparently watch over her, as a nursemaid might a child.

She hadn't been sure who to tell Clark to look out for, but it hadn't taken long for her to arrive.

The woman who stood within the doorway, however, was not at all what Madeline had expected.

"Hello," she greeted her enthusiastically, holding out her hand like any man would. "I'm Georgie."

Madeline stood and stared for a moment, and the woman just kept talking.

"Were you expecting a man? Most people are when they hear a detective named George is coming. But, here I am. I thought we could have a little meeting today, and then determine what you might need from me."

"Yes," Madeline finally managed. "Do come in."

Georgie stood a good head taller than Madeline, and while she wore a simple navy dress with a spencer overtop, somehow Madeline had the sense that she would be just as comfortable in a pair of breeches and linen shirt. She walked like a man, without the elegant grace of a lady, and Madeline wondered about who she was and where she was from.

But she pushed the thoughts from her mind; that was of no consequence to her and not at all why she was here.

"Please, have a seat," she said, waving her hand over to the table and chairs in the corner of the room, next to the bookshelves that held the many sculptures her father had collected over the years, causing her to miss him anew. He had always trusted her and supported her in whatever she did, believing in her like no other father believed in his daughter — at least from those she knew.

"Thank you," the detective said, looking completely out of place in such a setting.

"So, Miss Jenkins, is it?" Madeline asked, remembering how Drake had referred to her.

"Correct," Miss Jenkins said with a nod of her head. "But please, call me Georgie. Everyone does. Or Jenkins, if you prefer."

Madeline started, unable to imagine calling a woman — besides a servant, perhaps — by her last name alone.

"All right, then, Georgie," she said with a hesitant smile. "You may call me Madeline, then."

"I had already planned to, since we are to be such close friends and all," Georgie said with a wink that caused Madeline to laugh, if only in sheer surprise.

"Drake feels you are in danger," Georgie said, turning serious now. "Do you believe that to be true?"

Madeline sighed. "I do not think *I* am personally, no. I do, however, believe the business is."

Georgie studied her. "Please don't be insulted by this but... do you have any ability to look after yourself?"

"I—" Madeline paused, unsure of what to say. She had tried, and failed miserably. If Alice hadn't rescued her... she released her pride and accepted the offer. "I suppose I could use some help. At least until this is all sorted."

And, if Drake had other priorities — not that she blamed him — perhaps this Georgie could help her.

She had been wrong about one thing – Drake wasn't motivated by money, but by revenge. She understood that now.

"Will you also be helping Drake in determining just who is trying to discredit my business?"

My business. There. She had said it. Not her father's business, but hers — which it would be someday. She was determined that it be so.

"I will do what I can," Georgie said, her brown eyes studying Madeline in such a way that it seemed she learned everything about her with just one look. "Drake, however, is insistent that he remain involved. That he look after everything and ensure you are well..." she paused, "I think I understand why now."

Madeline had no idea what Georgie meant by that, but she smiled shyly anyway. "Thank you," she said, fidgeting with her hands, unsure of what to do now.

Georgie was so self-assured, so confident, and Madeline was aware that this was not a woman who would ever need protection from another. This was how she longed to be — a woman who was able to take care of herself, who didn't need rescuing by a friend, a father, a cousin, or a detective — male *or* female.

It was time that she take care of herself — to live the life she wanted. To take enjoyment when she could, such as sneaking away to the British Museum just because she wanted to.

There *was* one thing she wanted. One thing she could only take for herself.

"Actually, Georgie," she said, biting her lip as her heart

began to beat faster at what she was going to attempt. "There is something that I could use some help with. I wouldn't mind some accompaniment — although it will be in the middle of the night. Is that all right?"

Georgie grinned wickedly. "Actually surreptitious night visits are just my specialty," she said.

*   *   *

DRAKE WAS DOING all he could to push away the feeling of wanting — of wanting to be the one with Madeline, of wanting to solve her problems, of *wishing* that he could be in two different places at once.

But, for now, he would have to rely on Georgie to do for him what he couldn't.

For another report had come in, one of a big shipment that had recently been unloaded at the docks. A shipment that had not at all been legal, smuggled in from France, bypassing all of the taxes that should have been paid to the British government.

And he was supposed to deal with it.

When the Magistrate had told him of it with strict orders that he get to the bottom of it, and get to the bottom of it *now*, he most certainly hadn't shared the fact that it had all happened just under his nose, as he had been spending a great deal of time as of late at those very docks.

He just hadn't been paying attention to much besides Madeline. This only proved what happened when his focus wavered. He ran a hand through his hair as he made his way to the docks, purposefully choosing an alternate route so that he didn't have to pass Castleton Stone. Marshall was accompanying him today, for apparently this case, which involved money 'stolen' from the British government, was much more important than any murder or kidnapping or personal vendetta.

"What do you make of this?" Marshall huffed while attempting to keep up with Drake's long strides.

"There has been smuggling as long as there have been governments," Drake said with a sigh. "If they'd like to lessen it, they will have to lower the taxes and the restrictions on certain items."

"That's not going to happen."

"It's not. And therefore, smuggling. We'll ask around, determine if anyone has seen anything."

Marshall nodded, and they each went a separate way, agreeing to meet back in an hour. Drake wore no uniform, and yet he must have either been recognized or conducted himself with such an air that most of the urchins ran the other way when they saw him, with shouts of "a Runner!" on their tongues. Those that did talk to him had nothing to say, instantly suspicious of him.

The people here kept to themselves, and Drake knew they felt that to give up any information was a betrayal to their entire neighborhood, although Drake himself was one of them as much as any criminal was.

He was about to leave to meet Marshall and see if he had happened to have any luck, when he felt a tug on the back of his jacket.

"Mister?"

He turned to find a street-hardened child and was about to ask the young lad what he had stopped him for when he realized that the lad wasn't a lad at all, but rather a girl.

"Yes?"

"I hear yer lookin' for the smugglers."

"I am," he said slowly, not wanting to scare her off. This was the first anyone on the docks had even admitted to there *being* smugglers.

"If you want to find a smuggler, there is one thing you need to look for."

"Which is?"

She leaned in close, her voice dropping to a whisper.

"The hawk."

Drake's heart stopped. Before he could regain any thought, she turned and ran away.

"Wait!" he called, chasing after her. But she was too small, too swift, and before he could see where she went, she was gone.

CHAPTER 17

"Please don't look at me like that."

Georgie quirked an eyebrow. Tonight she was dressed just as Madeline had imagined would best suit her — in a white shirt tucked into breeches with boots that rose above her knees, a jacket around her shoulders, cinched in front with a button.

"Like what?"

"Like… I don't know, like I'm about to step foot in some bawdy house."

Georgie threw her head back and laughed, long and loud.

"Trust me, sweetheart, I've seen far worse than this. Actually, I believe it is quite bold of you and I applaud you for it. I can hardly wait to learn his reaction."

Madeline bit her lip.

She had never done anything like this before. When then-Lord Stephen Donning had been courting her, it had all been according to proper traditions, as was befitting an earl.

Even when it turned out that he had only trained to pose as one.

Madeline had soaked it all up. She had followed along,

enjoying the romance that had come with it all, believing that he had so desperately loved her.

It had all been a lie.

Now, with Drake... well, she was smarter now. She would *not* give her heart away.

But that didn't mean she couldn't have a little bit of fun. She knew he had stepped in a direction previously unknown to him when he had taken her to the museum. Now she was the one taking a step in an unprecedented path. Except that it was actually more of a leap.

She needed to prove that she was not the fragile little flower everyone thought her to be. That she was as strong a woman as Georgie, or Alice, or Rose. That she could look after herself and take what she wanted.

Tonight, she wanted Drake.

"You know where he lives?" she asked Georgie, who had hired a hack for the two of them and was escorting her through London to Drake's home.

"Of course I do," she said, tossing her head back. "He might not be aware that I do, but I make it my business to know everything about everyone I am associated with. And that includes Drake."

"Interesting," Madeline murmured, wondering if Georgie and Drake had come to know one another in a more... carnal sense.

Georgie must have read the question in her eyes. Was there anything that this woman missed?

She laughed long and loud. "The answer to your question is no. Drake and I are colleagues, and that is all. Perhaps friends at the most, but Drake... he doesn't let anyone come too close."

"He doesn't?"

"No." She shook her head. "His work is his life. It's his free time, his friends, his lover." She grinned mischievously.

"Except perhaps tonight."

Madeline's cheeks warmed. "I just want to talk to him."

"Right," Georgie said with a knowing smirk. "Can't say I've seen many 'just talks' at midnight."

Madeline ducked her head. Georgie was right, of course. At least, she hoped so. She had no idea how Drake was going to react to her appearance at his home.

But she was about to find out.

"Go have some fun," Georgie encouraged. "I'll be waiting."

"Oh, that's not necessary," Madeline said hurriedly, embarrassed at the thought of Georgie sitting out here in the carriage while she was inside with Drake.

"Tell you what," Georgie said. "Give me a wave out the window once you have sorted that you are staying for a time with Drake. Then I'll know you are in good hands. I'll return in a couple of hours."

Madeline reached out quickly and squeezed her hands. "Thank you," she said, then she pushed open the door of the hack and, as Georgie watched faithfully, stepped into the night and up the stairs into Drake's house, her heart hammering in time with her steps.

How embarrassing it would be if he rejected her and she was back in the hack with Georgie once more.

But she wouldn't know unless she tried.

* * *

DRAKE HEARD the roll of the wheels and the clip of the horse's hooves out his window but was surprised when it came to a sudden stop, the silence soon filled by a low murmur of voices. Women's voices. At this time of night, it was unusual to hear the soft sound of a female.

He knew that voice. What in the hell…

He shot out of his chair and ran to the window, peering

out to see Georgie waving to him from the hack below. He knew she couldn't see his expression, but he eyed her with chagrin. She was supposed to be watching out for Madeline. What was she doing at his house — and how did she even know where he lived?

He walked over to the door, wrenching it open. He was halfway down the stairs when he saw her.

"Madeline," he said, hearing the reproach in his voice, and her head snapped up.

"Drake."

"What are you doing here? Is everything all right?"

"I… Yes. No." She looked lost suddenly, and he realized he was being an ass.

"Come," he said, waving her back up the stairs and into the foyer. "Let's go inside before you are seen out here. Will Georgie be joining us?"

She gave a strangled laugh. "No. Not tonight."

She was dressed in dark grey, as though she was attempting to hide in the cloak of night.

Madeline looked completely out of place when she stepped into the small drawing room, and for the first time he wished that he had done more to make this home, rather than simply a place for work and to sleep.

"Where are all of your… things?" she asked, looking around.

"I have what I need," he said.

"Yes, but…"

"What did you expect?"

"I'm not sure," she said turning around. "Books, maybe. A blanket, a pillow. A table to set your tea."

"I don't drink tea."

"Yes, I can see that."

She turned and looked up at him, something burning in her eyes, something he had never seen before — and it stirred him. Gone was the scared woman who looked to others to help her, who hid behind her father's shadow. A different woman had appeared here tonight.

She walked over to the window, waving down below — to Georgie, quite obviously, and he wondered why his colleague had agreed to such a scheme, but the question fell away as he considered the woman in front of him.

Madeline's cloak and hood created an air of mystery around her. He couldn't help it. He needed to see more. He reached out and gently tugged the hood down, and as he did her hair slid around his fingers, freely tumbling in a silken waterfall around his hands. It did not break as he had thought it might. Rather it was soft. Flexible.

"What is your name?" she asked, suddenly.

"Drake." He arched an eyebrow.

"No. Your real name."

Ah.

"No one uses it. No one has since... my mother."

She waited.

He sighed. "Felton. It's Felton."

"Felton," she repeated, her face void of expression. "It... doesn't *not* suit you."

He couldn't help it. He laughed, and so did she, her face breaking into a true smile before the chuckle eased away.

"So, Felton Drake," she said tilting her head as she studied him, "who are you?"

He stopped short at the question. He had been so caught up in her beauty, the way her unbound hair glistened in the moonlight, that he had been only thinking of the future, of what could happen between the two of them.

He didn't want to consider her question, or what his answer might be. "I'm a detective."

"Outside of that."

"I—" he began but then realized he didn't have a way to answer her question. "I don't entirely know."

She stepped toward him, placing her hands on his chest, her fingertips brushing against him so lightly that they seemed to tickle, and he tried not to shiver.

"You have been helping others for so long that you have forgotten yourself," she murmured, and he captured her hands in his. "Tell me... what's important to you?" she asked, her words a whisper, a caress. "Close your eyes. What comes up?"

It seemed foolish, but the room was dimly lit enough that he did as she told him.

"Justice."

"But what else?"

He paused, searching deep within his soul, suddenly needing to answer her with a ferocity that he couldn't quite explain.

"Loyalty," he said gruffly. "Truth."

"Is there any*one* that means something to you?"

"My aunt and uncle," he said, not ashamed of that admission, "and—"

You. It was there, on his tongue, but he was still too afraid, too unsure to say it. How would she react? If he said it, if he put it out there into the world, it might take on a life of its own, a life that he would no longer be able to manage himself.

And yet... she was here. She had come to him.

So he took a chance. And instead of saying the word aloud, he bent his head and took her lips with his, telling her in another way just what he felt, just what he wanted to say but was too afraid to do so.

He reached up, trapping her jaw between his thumb and forefinger, angling her head so that he could better dive in and access her mouth. As his other arm splayed across her back, what began as a controlled searching, teasing, began to deepen, until he sensed the desperation that was beginning to seep out of him and into her. Could she feel it? What would she think of it? Would she realize just how much he wanted her — so much that it caused a pang in his chest like a slowly twisting knife?

But then she moaned and fisted her hands up in his hair, and he realized that he had nothing to fear, for she matched his desperation with her own.

She tasted like cream and sugar and temptation, and he longed to pick her up and throw her on the bed before showing her just exactly how he felt, how much he wanted to kiss every inch of her body before making love to her the best way he knew how, so that she knew she deserved to be honored and cherished and loved in a way that Maxfeld had tried to forever ruin for her.

But he didn't want to scare her. He had no idea what Maxfeld had done to her. He wished he could find the man and show him exactly what he thought of him, now that he knew Madeline and her sweet, gentle soul, but who knew where Maxfeld had run off to now. He might never find him.

Drake gripped Madeline's wrists, ready to move her back and away from him, to warn her that if they didn't stop now, he could make no promises as to where this might lead, but she wrenched her grip away and pushed him backward until the back of his knees hit the edge of the bed.

"Madeline?" he said in astonishment, lifting his head to see the bold determination that covered her eyes.

"I know what you are going to say," she said, her breath as ragged as his, rough, hard, and heady as she hovered over him. Gone was the fragile flower and in her place a blooming rose. "You are going to tell me that we shouldn't do this, that I should go home, that we must stop before it goes too far. But Drake... I *want* it to go far. That is why I'm here. I tried to do what everyone wanted me to do, to be the good girl, to follow in my father's footsteps, to marry a man that would elevate me to a position that so many women like me would do anything for. And look where it got me. But you know what? I'm glad. Because now I am utterly ruined and it doesn't matter what I do anymore. I have been trying to hang onto the business and even that is failing. So I am going to do what I please. Right now, that means doing this… with you."

She paused for a minute, biting her lip as she stared down at him, and he could tell that this had been a leap of faith for her — coming here, saying such things to him. She was scared, but there was no hesitation there. Her cheeks were a fiery red, her eyes blazing, and if desire had been simmering within him before, now it was flaming in bright, orange embers that could only be doused in one way. Then her confidence seemed to dip for a moment, flashing behind her eyes. "Er… that is, if you want to."

He propped himself up on his elbows, his eyes searching out hers. Once the two of them connected, it was as though the chain between them was so tight, so fierce, that he didn't see how it could ever be broken. It trembled with the tension that had gripped them from the moment she walked into this room. Except now instead of being awkward and unsure it threatened to explode.

Her movements were still tentative as she tilted her hips into him, and suddenly Drake didn't know how he could go another moment without having her in his arms, without knowing what she would feel like flush against him.

He worked his hands between them and untied the ribbons of her cloak, allowing it to billow to the ground behind her. She wore a simple dress, one with buttons down the back that did not take him long to undo. When the dress fell to the floor atop the cloak, he broke from her for a moment to appreciate the fact she was naked of any stays, her chemise the only thing remaining between him and a view of the delectable skin he knew was underneath.

"I knew I was coming to you so I ah… tried to dispense with some of the usual clothing."

"I'm glad of it," he said with a growl, dipping his head to find one of her breasts, nipping at it through the thin fabric of her chemise, wetting it so that he could see the pink of it beyond. The fire crackled, and he jumped slightly, the sound sending a tingle through him.

He pushed one strap over a narrow shoulder, then repeated the motion on the other side. The chemise fell to her waist, and he caught her to him, drawing her close as he tweaked one nipple while worshiping the other with his mouth. She moaned as she ran her fingers through his hair, dipping her head to rest it on top of his, and he felt like the luckiest man in the world to be given this chance to be with her, to be chosen by her.

"Madeline," he breathed, "you, love, are absolutely beautiful."

"You don't have to say that," she said, her words harsh, but he shook his head.

"You are. You must never forget it."

Her hips then made a play for his again, and he cupped her, slowly sliding one finger into her as his thumb came to the bud of her sex, and she tilted her head backward, her cry echoing around the near-empty room, and Drake told himself then that this was why he had left his chambers unadorned and unfilled — because they only needed one thing within, and that was Madeline.

He was ready to bring her to fulfillment, knowing she was almost there, but before he could do anymore, she pushed herself back, out of his arms, and stared down at him, her eyes damp with desire.

"What's wrong?" he asked, hearing the harshness in his own voice.

"You," she said, and for a moment he almost panicked, for the last thing he wanted was to be the cause of any further pain in her life. "You are completely dressed," she said, one corner of her lips curling upward. "We cannot have that."

She crouched down, and he nearly fainted — yes, him, fainted — at the sight of her naked body low before him. She untied one boot and then the other, throwing them across the room as though she was angry at them for keeping her from what she wanted. She climbed up him, then, until she reached the fall of his trousers, clumsily working at them until they were unfastened enough for the two of them to work together to slide them down over his hips. He sprang free, and she caught his length in her hand, causing him to grit his teeth as he tried to tamp down his need for her, to give her time to do as she pleased.

"Take your shirt off for me, will you?" she asked, and he nodded shakily before doing as she commanded.

She began to move her hand up and down, and when she looked up at him and met his gaze, she nearly broke him.

"Madeline," he managed, reaching down to try to escape her hand, but her grip was firm. "You don't understand," he said. "I need you now. All of you — if *you'll* have *me*."

When she nodded, he leaned down and picked her up before turning and laying her back on the bed.

"My turn now," he said with a wicked grin, and she reached up and held his face in her hands.

He positioned himself overtop of her, gripping one of her slim thighs in his hands as he lifted it to part her legs and give himself room to enter her — which he did with a swift plunge. So exquisite was the feel of her around him, her tightness, the way she gripped him deep within that he almost lost himself right there, but he forced himself to pause, to savor the moment as he also gave her time to adjust to him.

And then he began to move. He tried to be gentle, he truly did. But after two tender strokes, when she replied with an arch of her back and a request for more, his body took over, responding to hers with a ferocity the likes of which he had never before experienced.

"Madeline," he heard himself moan as he began to rock back and forth, no longer tender, but taking, naming her as his, showing her in every way he knew how that he was plundering her, taking all she had to offer and more.

She cried his name in return, and all the nerves in his body stood on end at the caress in her voice. He bent low over her, taking her mouth, kissing her neck, her temple, unable to keep himself away, needing all that she was and all that she had to offer. She matched his every thrust, and when she threw back her head, he knew how close she was. He flicked his thumbs over her nipples as he pounded into her ever harder, and suddenly she was convulsing around him as she cried out his name, and it let loose all he was holding back, from her and from himself.

He had never known a release like this, had never felt his entire body explode so entirely before going nearly completely numb.

When he finally came back to himself, he nearly collapsed on top of her, but managed to roll to the side, although he stayed beside her, unable to keep himself from touching her.

Their breath rose and fell in the same timing, and Drake couldn't help himself. He smiled. A sincere, deep smile. One that came from a place of true contentment. A place that he had not found himself in a very, very long time.

CHAPTER 18

Madeline could hardly believe what she had just done.

She had crossed London in the dead of night, had entered a man's chambers… and made love to him.

Well, she supposed he had made love to her, but either way—

And now, as he lay there looking at her with that goofy, amazing smile on his face, she knew it had all been worth it. Even if he never wanted to see her again. Even if this was just one night. Even if—

Before she could finish the thought or say another word, however, they both jumped when a loud thump resonated through the room.

"What in the—"

Drake was out of the bed and over to the window faster than she had ever seen another person move before.

"Get down," he hissed, as he lifted his head to see just who had disturbed them.

"Oh!" Madeline said, sitting up in the bed, bringing the

sheet to cover herself, although why, she had no idea. "That must be Georgie."

"Damn it, Georgie!" He cursed with such ferocity that Madeline nearly laughed.

"I wasn't sure about her when she first arrived," Madeline mused. "I was quite convinced that I didn't need anyone watching out for me, particularly another woman. But she is... most interesting, and I find I rather like her."

"Georgie *is* an interesting woman, that is for sure," Drake said, "but she has been there for me more times than I can count, and there are few I trust as I do her."

"She is your friend, then."

Drake paused. "I don't have friends."

"Well, it sounds like she is the closest thing to it," Madeline said gently, smiling at him.

He quirked an eyebrow, clearly uncomfortable with the conversation, although she appreciated that he wasn't shutting her out completely.

"Tell me, Madeline, just why we are speaking of another woman in this short amount of time we have together?"

"Because," Madeline said, rising from the bed and beginning to dress, searching out her chemise among the pile of clothes littered over the ground, "she is currently outside waiting for me."

"Fair point," he muttered.

After throwing her dress over her head, Madeline turned around so that Drake could fasten the buttons. Somehow, even after all that had just happened between them, this small gesture seemed so intimate that she had to clear her throat before she spoke.

"Will I... see you tomorrow?"

"You mean today?"

"Today, tomorrow... whatever you'd like to call it," she said, heat rising in her cheeks, shyness suddenly overwhelming her as the enormity of what she had just done washed over her.

"I shall come by and update you on the case," he said. "Georgie will be with you through the day to ensure nothing amiss occurs, and we have a man stationed at the factory tonight."

"Thank you," she said as she threw her cloak over her shoulders, and Drake stepped toward her, now clad in his unfastened trousers. "Here," he said, lifting his hands to her throat, picking up the ties in fingers that lightly brushed her skin, causing her to tremble all over again. "Let me."

She nodded, meeting his eyes as he tied a perfect bow. She turned before he saw too much, but just as she was about to pull open the door, her eyes fell on one of the few items in the room. At first, she thought that the round object sitting beside the lantern on the table by the door was a coin, but on closer inspection, it was something else — a pendant... with a familiar engraving.

She stopped, picking it up between her thumb and forefinger.

"This pendant," she mused, "I've seen this before."

"That's what everyone says," Drake said, although he took a few steps toward her, crossing his arms over his chest as interest overcame his features.

"My cousin has one just like this."

Drake's arms dropped to his side as he stood at full attention. Her words were like a bucket of cold water poured over his head.

"Like that? Your cousin Bennett?"

"Yes, I'm sure of it," she said, studying it closer, confused at his shock. "I remember remarking on the hawk. He seemed a bit embarrassed about it. When I asked him where it was from, he said it was from a club that he frequented."

"How long ago was this?" Drake demanded, crossing to

her, reaching up and wrapping his hands around her upper arms.

"Ah... I'm not sure. A few months ago, maybe?" she said, suddenly concerned about how intent Drake had become, his dark eyes flashing with an emotion she couldn't rightly identify, but he seemed upset.

"Is everything all right?" she asked.

"Not really," he said, shaking his head. "But I will get to the bottom of this."

"This is your father's pendant," she realized aloud, her eyes widening. "Why would my cousin have the same pendant as your father did, twenty years ago?"

"I don't know," Drake said, dropping his arms, "and that's what most concerns me. What did they have in common? What trouble does it mean?" He eyed her intently. "Madeline, you must promise me something."

"What is it?"

She didn't make promises anymore without knowing what they entailed.

"Please don't say anything to your cousin. Not until we can determine what this is about."

"But won't you want to ask him?"

"No," Drake shook his head, "not until I can determine more for myself."

"Very well," she said, though her eyes were troubled.

"Do you promise?"

She nodded hesitantly. She wasn't sure what caused her to choose loyalty to this man she had just met over the cousin she had known for her entire life, but if there was one thing she did know, deep within, it was that she could trust Drake. Perhaps not with her heart, but with information.

"I promise. Will you promise me something in return?"

He eyed her, crossing his arms over his chest. "Which would be?"

"Will you please tell me what you find out? I would not like to be surprised again."

He nodded curtly. "Very well."

A whistle sounded from outside, and Drake rolled his eyes as he opened the door for her. "Goodnight, Madeline."

"Goodnight, Drake."

* * *

Drake dressed all in black.

He should be going to bed. It was well into the middle of the night, and tomorrow would be another day of much to do.

But there was no way he was sleeping tonight.

Not after all that had just happened with Madeline.

And not after what he had just found out.

He picked up the pendant, pocketing it before he slipped from his room and down the stairs. He had nothing to hide from — not yet. He was a detective.

But not tonight.

Tonight, he was not working for Bow Street. He was working for himself, and for his parents. He was going to determine what happened to them — or, at least, what they had been involved in.

The answer lay at the docks, of that he was certain. What the Castletons had to do with it, he had no idea, but he could only hope that Madeline wasn't involved.

He didn't know what he would do if he found out that she had anything to do with this — although why she would admit to recognizing the pendant if she did, he had no idea. Was she trying to keep her enemies close?

The thought caused a sickening deep within him as he navigated the streets of London after dark, many eyeing him with the same suspicion with which he regarded everyone else. Was that why she had come to him? He didn't want to believe it, for their time together had seemed almost... magical, if he was the type to ascribe to such an idea.

Madeline was everything he could have ever asked for and more. Fire and passion had lurked deep within her, and his need for her had not been tamed but rather grew with a fury as all he wanted now was to see her again, to be with her again, to know her touch once more.

Madeline Castleton.

All thought her so weak and so frail.

How wrong they were.

For he had never known a stronger woman.

He could only hope that her strength and courage were fighting for all that was right and good.

He finally made it to the docks, passing by a dark Castleton Stone, noting the sentry he had ordered out front. The man didn't notice him and Drake continued on. He perused Powers' warehouse but there was nothing amiss.

Farther down was where he was likely to find any action — shipments that were unloaded in the dark of night, away from the eyes of all in the day.

He was about to continue down, following the Thames east when a sound caught his ear — one that was not at all ordinary not for this area at this time.

He switched direction, heading away from Powers' and back past Castleton Stone. On the other side of it was, as far as he was aware, a lumber yard. He had been there a time or two with his uncle, when his uncle had still hoped that Drake would follow in his and his father's footsteps and become a builder.

Drake chased after the noise like a dog on a scent, realizing that it sounded like the call of workers to one another — workers who shouldn't be here at this time of night.

The timberyard had a small warehouse on the one end

and Drake slipped as silently as he could next to it, moving a few pieces of lumber together to make a stepladder of sorts which he climbed on in order to see through the window. He could only hope that he wouldn't be noticed from within, but rather lost in the darkness of the night.

He squinted through the dirty glass. There were plenty of piles of building materials around the room. But there in the corner was a flicker of light, from what seemed to be a low lantern.

And around the lantern huddled at least five to six men, perhaps more lurking in the recesses of the room. Who were they and what were they doing here?

One rose and began pacing back and forth in front of the rest of them, seemingly providing instructions.

The others nodded and then began to follow him out.

Drake tried to descend his makeshift ladder but as he did one of the boards flew out from beneath him and tumbled to the ground. He jumped out of the way and avoided being caught in the fall but he cringed, knowing that the sound of the crash would have been impossible to ignore.

"What was that?" he heard being called from the other side of the wall.

"Not sure."

"Go check."

"Me?"

"Yes, you. Who else d'ya think it'd be?"

"I don' know, but—"

"Go."

The argument, at least, provided Drake with enough time to hide, and he dove behind a pile of brick, hoping that he would be concealed from view, that the man who had been reluctant to venture out on his own wouldn't have enough wherewithal to search too diligently.

Fortunately, he was right.

He could hear the footsteps from his hiding place, until sure enough they began to fade, with only the call of, "Nothing here! Must have been the wind," and he exhaled all of the air he had been holding deep in his lungs as he crept out and began to round the building, hugging the brick wall as he did so to keep from view.

Where were they? How could he hear voices but see nothing? It was preposterous. They could not have disappeared. They—

Then he heard something again, surprised to find that it was coming from practically under his feet. He crept over to the bank of the Thames, holding his breath as the stink of it washed over him. He was somewhat used to it, but there was nothing like being so close.

There — below him, was a cut out in the bank. It must be accessible from elsewhere, perhaps some secret tunnel — likely from within the building, he realized.

He leaned down to look below, not surprised to see that they were unloading a small boat. He couldn't be sure what was within the crates they carried, but he had an idea that whatever it was, it was likely contraband.

So here it was —the smuggling ring he had been sent to find. But did this have anything to do with the hawk pendant that was apparently tied to such a ring?

He pushed himself back from the bank, walking over to the door that faced the river itself, unsure of what he would do when he got there, but then he stopped short. For there, facing him, was a round circle on the door, with a familiar picture on the front of it — the very hawk that had been mocking him.

"Hey! You there!" he whirled around to see a man crossing from the Thames, closing in on him with each step. The lantern swung from one side to the other in front of him, until it finally cast enough light on his face for

Drake to see that the man approaching was no one familiar.

Drake scrambled back and away, turning and breaking into a run. He could not be caught here. Not yet. Not until he knew more about what his parents had to do with this operation.

But he would be back. And he was going to get to the bottom of this.

CHAPTER 19

The numbers swam before Madeline's eyes as she stared at the ledger book the next day.

She tapped her quill pen on her desk, the feather rising and tickling her nose.

It was mid-afternoon, and she still had not seen anything of Drake. Was he going to come today? Was he too busy? Was he unsure of all that had occurred between them last night? Did he think her wanton?

She groaned as she dropped her head onto the desk before her, covering her eyes with her hands.

"If I've ever seen someone in need of a tall drink, it would be you in this moment, Madeline."

She looked up to find Alice grinning down at her, flanked by Rose on one side and Georgie on the other.

"They didn't seem overly suspicious, so I allowed them in," Georgie said, sticking her thumb out at the pair of them. "I assume that was all right?"

"Of course," Madeline said with a sigh, waving a hand out in front of her. "Let's sit at the table."

"We are not sitting at the table," Alice said smartly. "We are here to take you away from your work."

"I've too much to do," Madeline argued, but Alice shook her head.

"You did not look as though you were doing anything when we arrived but feeling sorry for yourself. Besides that, Rose is only here for a few days more, and I know she would desperately love to see you."

Rose smiled and nodded, although Madeline was sure that she was only agreeing with Alice to be kind and because everyone always agreed with Alice — it was much easier that way.

"Why don't the three of us… " she looked over to Georgie, who grinned widely, "the four of us, that is, take a walk?"

"Along the Thames?" Rose asked, wrinkling her nose, and Alice inclined her head toward her.

"Perhaps that is not the best of ideas, but we are close to the Strand. We could stroll along there, see if we fancy anything."

"Have any of you ladies been to the Strand?" Georgie asked, raising an eyebrow, and Alice nodded.

"Of course we have. Do you propose we find someone to chaperone us?"

"I can take care of that," George said, opening up her jacket to reveal a band surrounding her torso, knives captured within it. The rest of them stared at her, their mouths open wide.

"Goodness," Alice said, the first to find her voice, as she always was. "Do you always walk around like that?"

"I do when it's my job to protect someone," she said with a nod toward Madeline. "Which it is at the moment."

"Well, Madeline," Alice said, turning her stare upon her, "it seems we have more to catch up on than I thought."

And so, as much as Madeline secretly harbored an inner

desire to sit around and wait for Drake, she told herself that this was much better — she was not the type of woman to wait for a man to come to her. It was why she had gone to him last night. Besides that, last night was a one-night-only event, a time for her to have some fun. She had no feelings for him besides the physical attraction and desire that she had sated in the candlelight.

Except... she was well aware of how untrue that thought was. For when she pictured him in her mind, she saw more than his muscular torso, the marks he bore which told a story of a man who had spent his life among the company of some less-than-savory types. In fact, it wasn't even what she saw — for anyone could take a look at him and his handsome, dark visage with stormy eyes and know that there was much lurking behind the surface.

No, the problem was how Drake made her feel.

Warm. Safe. Home.

Nothing that he would be particularly pleased to know.

"You seem... contemplative," Rose remarked, tilting her head to the side, and Madeline had the sense that there wasn't much that this woman missed.

"There has been much to contemplate," Madeline said with a smile.

"Do tell," Alice said, and Madeline began to share all new that had occurred since the dinner and billiards game, leaving out any mention of Drake besides his involvement in the case.

"Where is Drake now?"

"I'd like to know as well," Madeline said with a sigh. "He doesn't seem to be overly interested anymore."

"In the case or in you?" Alice asked with a smirk, to which Georgie snorted, although she covered it with a cough when Madeline eyed her with warning. If Alice found out about what happened last night, Madeline would never hear the end of it.

"Drake is complicated," Georgie finally said, and they all turned to the woman, who was receiving more than a few curious glances, dressed as she was in her breeches and jacket, a top hat covering her head, although she did not hide the fact that she was a woman with her hair in a low chignon beneath it. Madeline noted that while Alice and Rose hadn't remarked upon her appearance, they were obviously interested in who she was and what she was doing with Madeline.

"Georgie works with Drake," Madeline explained, and Alice's eyes lit up.

"You're a Runner!" she exclaimed, at which Georgie's gaze somewhat darkened, and Alice held up a hand. "I'm sorry — a detective," she said. "I had no idea there were women detectives."

"There aren't," Georgie answered with a gleam in her eyes. "Understood?"

"Of course," Alice said, although a smile danced on her lips, and Madeline was sure that there was already a story playing around in Alice's mind — one that she would soon be writing. Alice wrote nearly everything that came her way into a story, and was one of London's best-known novelists. "So, tell us about Drake."

"That's the thing," Georgie said. "It is hard to talk about Drake, for it is hard to know much about him. He doesn't say much about his past, although I am aware that he is still on the hunt for whoever killed his parents. But he doesn't let anyone in — at least, not often."

She eyed Madeline, who swallowed hard, aware that not much got by Alice.

"Madeline!" Alice cried, turning to her. "What happened?"
"Nothing."
"Madeline Castleton, something has happened," Alice

said, stopping in the middle of the street and running her eyes over Madeline from the top of her head to her toes, as though with such a perusal she would be able to ascertain whatever had occurred. "Tell me."

"I will," Madeline finally promised with a sigh. "But not here, not in the middle of the Strand."

Madeline looked around, noting that no one was paying them particularly much attention. St. Mary Le Strand towered in the distance, the cross atop the church looking over all of them while small groups of people passed, a horse and carriage clopping by and providing some coverage over their voices.

"You've been intimate with him!" Alice exclaimed, her guess accurate, before Madeline placed a finger on her lips and shushed her as a woman selling flowers looked at them with surprise.

"Enough!"

"Oh, do tell!" Alice said as Rose watched them with wide eyes, and Madeline looked at her with apology.

"You are likely most shocked and horrified by the two of us," Madeline said to her, raising her arms out to the sides. "I promise that we — at least *I* — was once quite respectable."

"But isn't it fun when you no longer are?" Alice asked with a laugh, and Madeline shot a dark look her way.

"Easy for you to say, married woman that you are now."

"Well," Alice said with a shrug, "perhaps you and Drake—"

"No."

The word came from both Madeline and Georgie at the same time, and Georgie eyed her with a look of apology.

"I'm sorry, Madeline," she said. "It is not my place to speak. But I'm glad that you are in agreement, that you are aware that Drake will never make a connection beyond anything fleeting and temporary. He is consumed by his work, and as much as I would like to see that change—"

"It won't," Madeline finished, caught by the way her very own words caused her stomach to fill with what tasted like bile, making her want to be sick. "I understand that. I have from the beginning."

"Good," Georgie said with relief. "I just... I like you, Madeline, and I don't want to see you hurt."

"Thank you, Georgie," she said, forcing a smile on her face, but when they began walking again, Madeline could see that Alice still seemed troubled.

"Are you sure—"

"I'm sure," Madeline said, placing a hand on her arm. "Now, what do you say we stop by Twinnings for a cup of tea?"

"I think that sounds like a perfect idea," Georgie said, and the four of them entered the shop, leaving all of their objections on the street behind them.

* * *

DRAKE STOOD outside the house that was more familiar than any other one in London, even his own. He flipped the pendant round and round in his fingers. His aunt and uncle would be home any minute, and he needed to speak to them. This time, he would get the answers he sought.

He had already been down to the timberyard once more in the light of day. It had been in full operation, with no one apparently the wiser of any goings on at night, nor any way to find out who was aware of what those might be. He had tried to find his way down to the small alcove on the bank, but without a partner to help him scale the side he could see no other way in, besides through the warehouse itself, and he wasn't going to find his way surreptitiously through there.

But he knew. He knew it was a smuggling operation.

Now, he just had to find out what his father's involvement with it had been.

While Drake had been at the docks, he had taken a moment to ask some of the workers about their pay, for guilt tugged at him for neglecting Madeline's case, but he was so close to solving his parents' murders, how could he stop now?

The workers had all told him the same — they had not received their paycheck for a couple of weeks until Madeline had been made aware and she had paid them herself. One of them had looked around, making sure that no one else could hear him, before he leaned into Drake, speaking quietly.

"There is something else."

"Oh?"

"We actually have been offered to be paid much more."

"By Castleton Stone?"

"No," the man shook his head. He was young, and hadn't seemed to have been working for the stone company for long. "We'd be paid if we *didn't* show up for work. But most of us are fairly loyal. Castleton's a good one, and we wouldn't want to leave his daughter stranded. But it's tempting."

Drake frowned.

"Who offered you this?"

The man shrugged.

"Can't be certain. It came as a letter to us all."

"Do you still have it?"

The man shook his head. "No. We were told to think on it and then we'd be contacted again soon."

"Thank you," Drake said, his thoughts in turmoil. "And please, don't go anywhere. Whoever is offering you this... it will not be legal nor long term. You've a good job here."

The man nodded, although said nothing as he continued on his way.

Drake sighed. He would go see Madeline and straighten

this all out. But at the moment, he had a visit of his own to make.

It was with a heavy heart that he knocked on his aunt and uncle's door.

"Aunt Mabel," he said when she opened it, almost wishing she wasn't here for what he had to say to his uncle.

She surprised him, however, when instead of inviting him in, she stepped outside and closed the door behind her.

"I know why you're here, Drake," she said, looking deeply into his eyes. "And I think your uncle is ready to share all."

"How did you—" He tilted his head as he studied her face, which had become quite contrite. "It was you. You sent me the package."

She bit her lip, finally nodding.

"Your uncle was adamant you not know the truth, and I agreed for a time, but when I saw that you would not let it go, I... well, I decided to help you."

"I'm glad you did," Drake said, relief washing over him that he would finally learn the truth. Before his aunt could let him into the house, the door swung open behind them and his uncle Andrew stood there with suspicion on his face, although he reached out and clapped a hand on Drake's shoulders.

"Come in, Son," he said, and led him into the sitting room while Mabel made herself scarce in the kitchen. His uncle let out a weary sigh as he eased his body into where it fit in its indent on the sofa. "You didn't let it go, did you."

It wasn't a question.

"I couldn't," Drake said helplessly. "I can't."

His uncle rubbed the bridge of his nose and sighed. "What do you need?"

"I need to know the truth," Drake said, sitting across from him, his elbows on his knees. He felt as weary as his uncle looked, and it was not just from the lack of sleep the night before. "How was my father involved with smugglers at the Hawk Club?"

His uncle's eyes widened, glistening with surprise.

"You know more than I would have thought possible."

"Of course I do," Drake said. "This is what I do for a living."

His uncle sat back, gripping the arms of the chair.

"It was all so long ago now."

"I know."

"Your father..." his uncle began, his lips twisting in a grimace, as though he wasn't sure if he should say what he was about to, "he always meant well. All he ever wanted was to provide for his family."

"But—"

"He worked for the timberyard near the Strand. You know the one, by the Stone building? Of course you do. If you know about the Hawk Club, you know about the building. Anyway. He didn't know it when he began, but the owner was a smuggler. The building company was a front, although they did some legitimate business as well. The man in charge, he would hire people, then assess their loyalty. If he approved them, he would bring them into his main business."

"Smuggling."

"Yes," his uncle nodded. "Your father moved up through the ranks, and soon he was the owner's second-in-command."

"What was the man's name?"

Drake kept his breathing even, steady, sure, not exposing just how much this knowledge was affecting him, not wanting to give his uncle any reason to hold anything back from him.

"Lee. Lee Fowler."

"What happened?"

"You were born. Your father decided that he wanted out, that he was done with it all, that he wanted to live a clean, legitimate life. Didn't want to put you in any danger, despite that the money he earned provided more than he could ever have imagined."

"Let me guess — he told this man Fowler that he wanted out."

"That's what he told me he was going to do," his uncle said, steepling his fingers in front of him. "I don't know what happened next. All I know is that he and your mother turned up dead. You were with us that night already. And here you stayed."

Drake couldn't sit still any longer. He stood and began to pace the room, back and forth over the worn wooden boards beneath his feet.

"Why would he do such a thing?" he finally asked, stopping and staring at his uncle in supplication. Andrew shrugged, lifting his large, meaty hands.

"He thought he was doing it for the right reasons. Wanted to create a good life for you and your mother."

"He could have done that without smuggling."

"Of course he could have," his uncle said sadly. "But he wanted something better for you."

"And instead, he *left* me," Drake said bitterly, "and killed my mother in the process."

"Now, Drake," his uncle began, but Drake was already shaking his head, backing away.

"Why didn't you tell me?" he asked, anger that had been carefully tamped down for so long beginning to bubble deep within him. "Why did you never say anything? All of those times I asked you, and you said nothing, wouldn't tell me anything, and you knew all along. I trusted you."

"I was trying to protect you," his uncle said, standing himself now, his face wreathed in concern. "I knew that you would try going after him, and I couldn't have that. I didn't want you to end up like your parents."

"That would be my own choosing," Drake said, his jaw tightening. "I'm a grown man."

"I know that," his uncle said with a heavy sigh. "And there is nothing I can do about that now. I still would have made the same decision not to tell you. I know I cannot keep you from going after them, Drake, but I would ask you a couple of things."

"Go on," Drake said, wanting to say that his uncle had no place to ask him, not when he kept such information from him, but this was the man who raised him. He had to give him the chance to at least say what he needed to.

"Don't go after him alone. And please, please, Drake — be careful."

Drake nodded.

"I will try," he said and then turned on his heel and nearly ran out of the house.

CHAPTER 20

Madeline tapped her pen on the table as she looked at the calendar in front of her.

Her father was going to return in a week's time. She should feel joy at the idea, and part of her, deep within, most certainly did. He was her entire family and she loved him more than anyone. She had missed him terribly and could hardly wait to see him.

And yet if he arrived before this was all over… he would think that she couldn't handle this, and would never give her the opportunity she desperately wanted.

She dropped her head into her hands, covering her face. Would anything ever start going right for her?

"Well, well, it looks like we are still feeling sorry for ourselves."

Madeline jerked her head up and shot to her feet.

She must be daydreaming — or having a day-mare. Was that a word? Not that it mattered. For, she was afraid, this was all too real. She pinched herself. Yes, it was true. There he was, sitting in front of her, as though he had been conjured by some evil spirit.

"What are you doing here?" she bit out to the one man she had never wanted to see again. The one man she wished had disappeared from her life forever was here. In her office. No, her father's office, she reminded herself.

"That's hardly any way to greet one's husband, now is it?"

Karl Maxfeld, the man who had pretended to be her husband in order to win her fortune, grinned at her with that smile that at one time had drawn her in, had tempted her and promised her everything she had thought she had wanted.

Now it sickened her.

"You are not my husband. You never were. You had another wife — or three — before me."

"That I do," he said, "but that doesn't mean I don't still feel something for you."

"The only thing I feel for you is disgust," she practically snarled. "Now, get out."

"Or else what?" he laughed. "You're going to send the Runner after me? He's not here right now."

"No, but—"

"She's not here either," Maxfeld said, winking at her. "She was sent off on an…errand."

"What did you do to her?" Madeline demanded, fear rising in her chest.

"Why, nothing at all," he said, feigning innocence, "just told her about a scuffle down the way, over at the timberyard. We only have a few minutes until she returns, so let's make this count, now, shall we?"

"I shall not be happy until you are gone and out of my life forever — which I thought you were."

"Oh, but I can be!" he exclaimed. "And I can actually help."

"Never."

"Not so fast," he said, waving a finger back and forth in front of his face. "I hear you've been having a little trouble."

She eyed him warily. "So you are behind it, then."

He sighed. "Alas, I cannot take the credit, for I was in Newgate when this all began. But I hear things. And I know things. I know you need help."

"I have help."

He snorted. "Fat lot of good that is doing for you."

He was right, although she had no desire to admit it.

"I'll tell you what, Madeline," he said. "If you pay me what I deserve — what I should have received — then I will fix everything."

"What you deserve?" she exclaimed, unable to help the rise in her voice, "you mean what you would have received upon my *death*?"

She wished Drake were here. He would know what to do, could arrest Maxfeld, and get her out of this mess.

But he was otherwise occupied, with something much more important than her. And it was no fault of his own — she had been well aware of how he truly felt when she went to him last night.

Even though she was beginning to realize that *she* felt entirely different. She cared for him, far more than she ever should.

"Get. Out." She pointed to the door. "Get out and stay out and never come back."

"Very well," he said with a sigh. "How about a kiss goodbye, to remember our past?"

She rounded the desk, drew back her hand, and before she even realized what she was doing, slapped him across the face.

His eyes darkened, then narrowed as he advanced upon her. "You're going to regret that."

A spark of fear sprang in her breast. She was in the middle of her factory, and if she screamed, she could only hope that someone would hear her, but—

"What do you think you are doing here?"

Her question was repeated, but this time by a new voice.

"Bennett," she said, trying to keep the relief from her voice. "Would you please escort out my... visitor?"

She nearly choked on the word, but she had no idea how to describe him.

While tall and thin and not at all menacing, Bennett was, at the very least, another presence in the room.

"With pleasure," he snarled. "Come, Maxfeld."

He walked over and grabbed his arm, but Maxfeld shook it off. "I will go willingly. No need to escort me out like a woman."

Madeline snorted, but Bennett thankfully didn't let go, and wrenched Maxfeld out of the office and away from Madeline.

When they left, she sank into her chair, relief filling her. She didn't know how long she sat there, stunned at the entire affair, until Bennett returned.

"Madeline, are you all right?" he said, crossing over to her, and she nodded shakily.

"I think so."

"I can hardly believe he would show his face here," Bennett snarled. "And of course, he would come when one of your Runner friends was absent."

"He did that by design," Madeline said, twining her fingers together, wishing that she could be stronger, that she didn't always have to rely on others to fight her battles for her. "Thank goodness you came when you did."

"Of course," Bennett said, sitting down across from her and leaning forward, staring at her intently. "Madeline, you know that I will always be here for you."

"I know," she said with a small, forced smile, for he only further proved that she could not stand on her own. "I appreciate it."

"I had a thought," he continued, rubbing his temple as

though he was unsure of whether or not he should say it aloud, but she encouraged him to continue. "Your father has always believed that you are the best person to continue to look after this business when he is finished with it."

"Yes," she replied, suddenly wary as to what Bennett was about to propose.

"However, there have been… occurrences that have arisen since he left to Bath."

"Yes, there have been," she acknowledged, but then couldn't help but add, "Although most have not been under my control."

"A fair point," he said, lifting a finger. "However, you know they always say that you're only as strong as your leader."

"What are you trying to say, Bennett?"

"I'm trying to say that while you may be more than capable, a woman will never be fully respected to run a business. It is no fault of your own, but that is just the truth."

Madeline said nothing, becoming more irritated with him as he spoke.

"What I am proposing is that we, perhaps, partner together. I can be the face of the business. I will negotiate, take meetings, discuss projects with clients. You can do what you do best — keep the ledgers, ensure the business is running smoothly, and create the sculptures that you love so much."

Madeline tapped her quill pen on the table. She hated to admit it, but his offer was tempting. She had missed sculpting, and she obviously was struggling to have anyone believe that she, as a woman, could effectively run Castleton Stone.

"So would we be partners, then?"

He hesitated, tilting his head to the side.

"Well, I would likely need to be in command. You could be… an assistant of sorts."

Madeline pushed herself back in the chair so that every inch of her spine was connected to the back of it.

"Oh, would I?"

"Yes," he said with a nod and a smile, seemingly pleased with himself. "Similar as you are now for your father. I think it would be quite an effective arrangement."

Madeline held her tongue. She was pleased she had never been the type to say exactly what she thought, although in that moment she wished she knew the right words to tell Bennett what he could do with his idea.

"I will take what you have suggested, and I will think on it," she said calmly. "But ultimately, this is my father's decision."

A flash of panic crossed Bennett's face. "Yes, but if you suggest it to him, then—"

"Thank you, Bennett," she said curtly. "You may go."

A footstep from the hall caught her attention, and she turned to find Drake lounging in the doorway.

"You," Bennett said, standing abruptly. "Have you been eavesdropping?"

"I am awaiting my turn to speak with Miss Castleton," he said smoothly, but Madeline could tell that there was turmoil lurking behind his eyes.

"Very well," Bennett said, narrowing his gaze at first Drake and then Madeline, as though he suspected something, although what, she had no idea. He left with one final glance over his shoulder, and Drake crossed the room and shut the door behind him.

"What are you doing?" Madeline asked, standing up and placing her sweaty palms on the desk in front of her. "Georgie is set to return at any moment."

"She's not," Drake said. "When she realized she had been set up, she returned, found you here with Bennett, and then sent a boy to fetch me to come."

"I am glad that I was deemed important enough to leave whatever had you occupied," Madeline said, but then instantly regretted her words. "I'm sorry. I had no right—"

"No, you did," Drake said with a sigh, rounding the desk to stand in front of her. He lifted his hands to wrap them around her upper arms and his voice was nearly hushed. "I have neglected you, and for that, I am sorry."

"It's not your fault," she shook her head. "You have much else that requires your attention."

He lowered his hands, as well as his head so that she could no longer see his expression. "I believe I know who murdered my parents."

"You do?" she said in shock, suddenly feeling ridiculous for even suggesting that her trouble was worth his time. Thoughts of Maxfeld fled at his revelation.

He nodded slowly. "It seems my father was involved with a smuggling ring. He tried to get out, but the organization feared that he would talk. So, one night, they killed him — and my mother too."

Madeline couldn't help her jaw from dropping open. "You didn't know that he was involved?"

"I didn't," he said, shaking his head. "My uncle did. My aunt too. She was the one who sent me the satchel, and who finally encouraged my uncle to tell me all that he knew. If only he had done so earlier."

Bitterness leaked into his tone, but Madeline welcomed the sharing of his emotion and she grasped his hands in hers. "I'm sure he thought he was protecting you."

"That's what he said." Drake laughed sharply. "You all sound the same."

"Drake," Madeline said slowly, "people have been protecting me my entire life. I know this might not be what you want to hear, but it does mean that you are loved."

"There is more," he said, ignoring her, obviously still unwilling to navigate his own emotions.

"Yes?"

"I believe your cousin is involved."

"What?" she gasped, nearly unable to comprehend just what he was saying. "In the *smuggling* ring?"

"Yes, the smuggling ring," he said with a nod. "The pendant you said he had — it's the pendant that every member receives. It's the pendant required to enter their headquarters — which is right next door."

"Next door?" she echoed, "To here?"

"The timberyard," he said with a nod, spreading his fingers out on the desk, and Madeline closed her eyes as she tried not to notice how big and strong they were, tried not to remember what they felt like upon her skin. "It is a front for the smuggling ring. They use the docks at night."

Madeline shook her head, unable to take in all that he was saying. "It couldn't be," she argued, even though she knew that Drake had no reason to lie to her. "I would know. My father would know. And as for Bennett—"

"The man who wants to take your job, who wants to run the business instead of you?"

"So you *were* eavesdropping," she murmured.

"I was waiting at the door," he countered. "Neither of you heard me. But it only proves his part in all of this. He wants Castleton Stone, Madeline. And I believe he wants it for its proximity to the smugglers. Your father may not have known about it, but you would have found out eventually. Especially with me around at the moment."

He gave her a small, sad, half-smile that said more than his words ever could.

"At the moment?"

"Until this is solved," he said, turning away from her, shutting her out. "Then I'll be out of your life."

Madeline opened her mouth and then closed it again. She was desperate to cry out to him, to tell him not to leave her, but what could she possibly say? They had no understanding. No reason to be together. And yet—

"It... it doesn't have to be goodbye," she said, her words just above a whisper. "I mean—"

He turned around quickly, any thought or feeling he might have had wiped clean from his features. "When you came to me last night, Madeline, I was clear that I could not give you a future. We had a moment in time together. A moment that I will always remember, yes, but that's all it was. It cannot be more, do you understand?"

"But..." Madeline swallowed the lump in her throat, blinked back the tears that threatened, "why?"

"There is no room in my life for a woman," he said, with a shrug of his shoulders. "Not even you."

He looked her in the eye. "I made love to you because I thought you understood. Because I thought you were the same — that you didn't want anything beyond what we could have for that one night."

"I—" her voice was hoarse, but she forced herself to say what she felt, even though the realization of her feelings arose as she spoke. "I thought that was what I wanted. I really did. But you... you have stolen a piece of my heart, Drake."

When he met her eyes then, his were dark, glassy, and she couldn't tell whether he was angry or upset or frustrated, but all she wanted was the return of the man that had held her close, who had told her he would take care of her and be everything she needed.

"Why are you being like this?" she finally burst out, flinging her hands to the side.

"I'm only being honest, Madeline," he said, his words stark and void of emotion. "Isn't this what you want? Someone who will treat you like a grown woman? Someone who doesn't pity you, but respects you enough to tell you the truth? That is what I am doing. You were naïve about Maxfeld, yes. I thought you had learned from it. But if you refuse to see the truth about your cousin, then perhaps you are the ignorant little girl everyone thinks you are."

Madeline stared at him, her mouth and eyes both open wide as shock invaded. Finally, she caught hold of her senses.

"I am currently running Castleton Stone. How many women do you know who find themselves in such a position?"

He lifted an eyebrow. "Yes, and how well has that been going?"

Madeline couldn't breathe. It was as though Drake had taken a knife and plunged it deep into her stomach before twisting it and holding it in place.

She set her jaw.

"Get out."

He inclined his head. "I'll remain here to catch Bennett in the act. Then I will go. I will—"

"I said *get out*," Madeline said through clenched teeth. "That means get out of my office, get out of my factory, get out of Castleton Stone. You are not welcome here any longer. I made a mistake coming to you, but that will be the last one I will ever make. I will send payment to Bow Street."

"Madeline," Drake's voice softened somewhat, "I will make sure that—"

"*Leave*," she said forcefully, needing him gone before she lost all control. "Leave now."

He stared at her for a moment longer before finally nodding at her, turning on his heel, and walking out the door.

Madeline followed him, slammed it behind him, and managed to make it to a chair before she folded over and let the tears fall.

CHAPTER 21

Drake's heart had been ripped from his chest.

And he had done it to himself.

He wished he hadn't had to push it so far. He wished that he had been able to break things off cleanly, without hurting Madeline to such an extent.

But it had been necessary. He needed her to stay away from him. And so he had used the words he had known would work. The words that would keep her away. But also the words that had completely broken her, and him in turn.

He hadn't known it was possible for this pain to ever invade again. It was why he kept everyone away. Why he had tried to shield himself from Madeline. But somehow she had broken through the walls he had so carefully constructed, finding her way in.

Now, he didn't know how he could live with himself, knowing what he had done to her.

But it was better than living in a world without her in it — which was most certainly a possibility if they stayed together.

"Drake!"

He turned around quickly to find Georgie running after him. She was wearing her trousers and jacket today but with her hair visible behind her, her feminine features and apparent curves, there was no mistaking her for a man.

She caught up to him, still in control of her breath despite her sprint. "What happened?" she asked.

He ran a hand through his hair. "It's over," he grunted, looking off into the distance, unable to meet Georgie's shrewd, knowing gaze. "I told her that what we had was a moment in time and that there could never be anything more between us."

"She wanted there to be?" Georgie asked, lifting her eyebrows, her gaze interested although not judgmental, which he appreciated.

"I'm not sure if she knows what she wants either," he muttered, looking away, down the docks in front of them. "But I can't have her near me. I had to push her away... as much as it hurt both of us."

"What exactly did you say?"

The sounds of workers across the street, unloading cargo from the ships, reached them and Drake took a breath as he watched them, considering how much simpler his life could be if he had a job like that, but also aware that every person held their own troubles, their own issues, and nothing was ever perfect.

"I told her that she was naïve. That she wasn't fit to run Castleton Stone."

Georgie's mouth dropped open. "You didn't."

"I had to," Drake said, his words anguished, and Georgie's expression softened, as though she realized now just how much it had hurt him to say what he did.

"Georgie... my mother was murdered because of my father's involvement this gang. She was associated with him, and it killed her. You know better than anyone how much danger we find ourselves in from day to day. Now that I am looking into my parents' murder, there is just as great of a chance that whoever killed them will come after me, and in turn Madeline. I can't have her involved. I can't put her at risk."

"It seems to me that the woman is something of a survivor."

"Yes, she is. But she doesn't need to be put in any more danger because of me."

Georgie was silent for a moment, heaving a sigh as she placed her hands on her hips and looked off into the distance. "Well, then, I think you know what you must do."

"Which is?"

"Solve this murder. Take down this smuggling ring. You know I will help you. Marshall will too. Then you can go back to Madeline."

"I don't think she'll have me."

"You can do nothing but try."

He nodded. "Let's focus on the first bit. Here is what I am thinking."

He then pushed Madeline as far from his mind as he could, while making a plan with Georgie.

"Will you keep an eye on Madeline while I find Marshall? She doesn't want any of us around anymore, but I would feel better if you were here."

"Of course," Georgie said with a nod. "She's a stronger woman than you think, though, Drake."

"I know she is," he said, fervor in his voice, "and if anyone needs to learn that it's her."

"I'll keep an eye out," Georgie promised. "See you tonight."

***

MADELINE DIDN'T KNOW what to do with herself. She couldn't stop thinking about Drake, about all he had said, and all of his accusations.

She had thought that he was the one person who understood. She had thought that no matter what else, he would be there for her, supporting her. She had thought that he had believed in her.

She had been wrong.

When the numbers on the ledgers in front of her wouldn't stop swimming through her watery eyes, she finally threw the cover of the book shut and abandoned it completely.

There was only one thing to do when she felt like this, one thing that would bring her some solace, and hopefully some peace.

The other artists greeted her with a smile when she arrived at their corner of the factory. She forced a returning smile to her face, but they seemed to sense her mood.

If there was ever anyone who understood that she didn't always want to talk but rather had to work things through with her hands, it was these people before her.

Thomas said nothing. Instead, he rose, walked over to the back of the factory where the vats of clay were stored, and set a heap of it on the table in front of Madeline.

She looked at it for a moment.

"This isn't the usual clay."

"It's your new formula." Clark, who had long been with Castleton Stone, said from behind her. "You left your notes out the other night. I know how hard you've been working on it, so... I thought we should try it."

His smile was both hesitating and conspiratorial.

"You should be the first to sculpt with it," Thomas said with a serious nod, and Madeline could only blink.

"Thank you," she said, before her focus turned to the stone itself.

She didn't know how long she sat there and stared at it, until she grabbed an apron and wrapped it around herself.

Thomas gave her no instructions, no special orders. He seemed to know that she needed to create something for herself, even if she didn't know what that was going to be quite yet.

She stood, closed her eyes, wet her hands, and ran them over the clay, feeling it, testing it, shaping it, allowing it to tell her what it was to be transformed into. It had been so long since she had sculpted based on her passion alone, so long since she had looked at it as art rather than work.

But today, she needed it.

So she released all of the feelings, all of the thoughts. She let go of Maxfeld. Of Bennett. Of Drake.

And she sculpted.

* * *

MARSHALL GREETED Drake at Bow Street with a nod. "I have news."

"Oh?"

"You're about to be very happy with me."

"Am I, now?" Drake said with a raised brow, causing Marshall to chortle. Drake was never happy with him.

"I've found something out," Marshall said, his smile fading, and Drake's heart began to stutter at his now-grave expression. "We had an informant come forward."

"From where?" Drake said, not wanting to get his hopes up, but unable to tamp them down completely.

"From the timberyard. The Hawk Club."

"And?"

"The man says no names. Wants to be released, helped out

of the city. It seems he's the father of the young girl who gave you information the other day. She told her father what she did. Luckily, he's the sort that, at the very least, didn't do anything to the girl, but he's smart enough to know what's best for him and his family."

"What did you tell him?"

"It's with the Magistrate, but I have the information."

"Which is?"

"I know who killed your parents."

Drake's heart completely stopped then, until finally it resumed, booming so loudly in his ears that it nearly drowned out everything else Marshall said. "He's the owner of the timberyard."

"Lee Fowler," Drake said, and Marshall nodded in surprise.

"You knew?"

"My uncle told me the name of the man who led the smuggling ring," he said bitterly. "It was a guess. Where is he now?"

"At the timberyard, I would suppose," Marshall said with a shrug, and Drake had already turned and was halfway out the door when Marshall rose and began to come after him.

"Where are you going?"

"Where do you think I'm going?" Drake said gruffly when Marshall finally caught him, trying to pull him back.

"What are you going to do?" Marshall said. "You can't just run down there alone. Will you take on him and the entire gang with your bare hands?"

"If I have to."

"That is ludicrous!" Marshall said. "I'll go back for some help. Will you wait for me?"

"Yes, go," Drake said, becoming impatient, but the moment Marshall left, he took off himself, fetching his horse from the stables so that he could be on his way quickly.

This was not the work of Bow Street. He had to take this on himself.

* * *

The dock workers had finished their shift by the time Drake returned to College Street. He ignored Castleton Stone as he passed, instead making his way to the timberyard. He was not going to shy away from what awaited him, and so he walked right up to the door and knocked.

A tall, burly man opened the door to him.

"We're closed," he said, beginning to shut the door, but Drake stuck his foot in it so that he couldn't do so.

"I'm here to see Lee Fowler."

"Not in."

Drake took the man by surprise when he stepped forward with his shoulder and heaved the door open. The man fell back slightly and with the advantage of surprise Drake fit through the gap in the door.

The room wasn't much, but held a desk in one corner and a glimpse of a hallway to the back.

"Where is he?"

"Not here, I told you."

"It's all right, Anderson." A voice emerged from the recesses of the room. "Let him in."

Drake turned slowly to face him.

"Do you know who I am?"

"I do… Drake."

"I need to speak with you."

"I'm not in the habit of speaking with Runners."

"I'm not here from Bow Street. Not today"

"Oh?" Fowler raised an eyebrow. "Well, then, come right in."

He crooked a hand at him, and Drake knew it was not

wise to follow alone into the other man's space upon a sarcastic invitation, but he no longer cared. It didn't matter what happened to him anymore. Madeline wouldn't want him. His aunt and uncle would miss him, sure, but they didn't necessarily *need* him.

While he needed this. He needed revenge. He needed to make things right.

With any luck, Marshall and the other detectives would be here soon, but first, Drake would find the truth.

Fowler led him down a set of stairs, into darkness, and when Drake heard the splash of water, he knew exactly where he was. They were nearing the opening to the Thames.

He also suspected what Fowler intended to do with him.

"So tell me, Drake, is this what you are here for?"

Fowler lit a lantern and allowed light to flood over the room, illuminating cases and barrels and crates, full of what Drake was sure were illegal, smuggled goods.

"This is what Bow Street wants. What the Crown wants," he said.

"But not you?"

The lantern shone on Fowler's smug expression, and Drake slowly shook his head.

"I want something else."

"And just what is that?"

"Justice."

"Justice?" Fowler laughed, the light-blond hair on his head hardly moving. "For what?"

"You know for what," Drake practically growled. "For my parents."

"Your parents?" Fowler said, as though he had to think hard to remember them. "Ah, your *parents*. That's right. I thought the name Drake was familiar. Your father… he was a good worker. A partner."

"And you killed him."

Lee folded his arms across his chest, allowing his jacket to open as he did so, showing Drake the firearm at his side.

"What do you think about loyalty, Drake?"

Drake said nothing. He didn't have to share any of his thoughts with this man.

"Well, I'll tell you what *I* think," Fowler said. "Your father was going to betray me. I couldn't have that. There is nothing worth more than loyalty."

"And my mother?"

Fowler waved his hand in the air. "Wrong place, wrong time, and all that. I didn't know she was here until it was too late. Seemed she followed your father in, wanted to see what he was doing. Well, she saw too much."

Drake growled as Fowler reached into his jacket. "Unfortunately, Drake, you've gotten yourself into the same situation."

As Fowler began to lift his hand, Drake didn't hesitate.

He lunged, not needing a weapon, for his rage alone was enough to carry him through.

Drake's fist met Fowler's face with such sickening ferocity that it nearly surprised himself, and Fowler went flying backward.

He managed to take two more swings on the man before he was grabbed from behind, pulled backward by men that he hadn't even noticed, just as the door burst open.

"Drake!"

It was Marshall, along with Georgie, looking back and forth between Drake and Fowler. Luckily their guns were drawn, and Fowler's had been knocked loose in the scuffle. He was now holding his nose, dripping blood down his shirt.

"This man assaulted me!" Fowler said, pointing at Drake, who shared a look with Georgie and Marshall as Georgie rolled her eyes.

"If he did, you deserved it," she said. "Let's go, Drake."

She gestured to the door.

He hesitated. Fowler deserved to suffer much more than a bloody nose.

But what he had to do, he would do alone, without bringing Marshall and Georgie into this.

Drake did as she said, but the look he cast over his shoulder told Fowler that he would be back — and that things were going to end much differently next time. Of that, he was sure.

CHAPTER 22

Madeline didn't know what time it was.

She did know she was alone. Thomas had laid a gentle hand on her shoulder a few hours ago and told her that the rest of them were leaving for the night. She had nodded, promising that she would be just a few more minutes. Thomas told her that he would let Bennett know that she was still here, to make sure she wouldn't remain at the factory alone.

Her rumbling stomach was the only reminder of how long it had been. She finally lifted her head, rolling her neck and her shoulders, which had become cramped from remaining in the same position, bent over the sculpture for so long now.

She stared down at it.

And looked into Drake's face.

She sighed, dropping her head into her hands, rubbing her eyes with the heels of them.

She had wanted nothing more than to come down to the factory, to return to what she loved, and completely forget about him. But instead, she had carved him into her new stone. He wouldn't leave her mind no matter what she did.

Finally, she allowed her thoughts to return, and they began to wander over all that he had said, all that he accused her of, all that he had mercilessly hurled at her.

And she began to wonder. Did he really think such things? Or was he only trying to drive her away?

She had thought that she was finally breaking her way through the walls she knew were firmly in place around him. At least she had learned why he had erected them in the first place.

But in the process of her offensive, she had left her own subject to attack.

Those barricades she had so carefully put into place, to keep herself from ever being hurt again — he had found his way in, through holes that she hadn't even known were there.

Then he had taken advantage of his position and he had destroyed her.

She hated him for it.

And yet... the only reason he had been able to hurt her so was because of how much she loved him.

She shouldn't. She should be glad that he was gone, should despise him with every fiber of her soul for the things he had said to her.

Except... Drake hardly ever showed emotion. Ever. Yet when he said those things to her, it wasn't anger or malice that lurked behind his eyes.

No.

It was pain. He was as hurt as she was by his words.

So why, oh why, had he said them?

She didn't know. But she had to find out. And there was only one way to do so — to ask him.

Madeline looked down at the sculpture in front of her.

"I'll get through that thick head of yours, one way or another," she whispered, closing her eyes and tilting her head back as she stood and threw her arms out, stretching her stiff muscles.

Then she turned, opened her eyes, and screamed.

* * *

Drake had nearly fought Marshall and Georgie as they led him out of the timberyard.

"What are you doing?" he asked, wrenching himself away. "I had him. The man who murdered my parents."

"And what were you going to do to him?" Georgie asked, throwing her hands out to the side. "You had no weapon out, and they outnumbered you at least four-to-one."

"The three of us could have done something," Drake grumbled.

"Yes, we could have," Marshall said, his mustache quivering in his ire, "if you had only waited for me."

"Now they know we're onto them, and sure enough they are likely loading up all of the stolen goods in their warehouse and will have them on a boat within hours, leaving us nothing to find, nothing to come after them for."

"Then we strike now," Drake insisted. "It doesn't have to be according to what Bow Street says. This is personal."

Georgie tilted her head as she looked at him. "We understand what this means to you. We're your friends, and we want to be there for you. But—"

She and Marshall shared a look, and she bit her lip as she turned back to him. "We've been told that we are to bring you back to Bow Street to speak with the Magistrate."

"About what?"

"Well," she exhaled audibly as she placed her hands on her

hips. "He feels this has become too personal for you. He wants you to take some time."

"Time?"

"Time away. Away from the case. Away from work," she said.

Fire began to race through Drake. "Never."

"We're not going to forcibly bring you in, Drake," Georgie said softly.

Drake looked around as he ran a hand through his hair.

"I'll go on my own," he promised. "But I suggest that you get some help, and then return and take them down now."

"He's right," Marshall said to Georgie before turning back to Drake. "Do you promise to leave?"

"No," Drake said, shaking his head. "But I will not go inside. I will wait and watch until you return."

"And if anything happens?"

"I'll send one of the urchins to come and get you."

Marshall eyed him suspiciously, but finally shrugged.

"Very well."

They turned to go, when Drake suddenly whipped his head back toward Georgie.

"Where's Madeline?"

"I'm not entirely sure," Georgie said. "Likely home by now."

"Likely?"

"Well, Marshall came to get me to come help you. Madeline had been sitting in the factory for hours at that point, working on some sculpture. She was surrounded by everyone who worked with her, so I figured she was less at risk than you were."

Fear began to claw at Drake's throat.

"Who was still there when you left?"

"I don't know," Georgie said defensively. "A couple of the sculptors and her cousin."

"Her cousin?" he burst out. "Georgie—"

But he stopped. It wasn't Georgie's fault. She had no idea that Bennett might be part of it. And, for all he knew, he was wrong. He had never proven Bennett to be connected at all. He let out a breath.

"Very well. Thank you, Georgie."

"Are you all right, Drake?" she asked, looking at him with concern, and he managed a quick nod.

"Fine."

"We'll be back," she promised. "Don't do anything stupid."

The sun was just beginning to set, and Drake ran his hands through his hair. It seemed like everything he did these days fell into that category.

He had promised not to go into the building — but he had never promised not to venture into the timberyard. He could only hope that Madeline would be home by now, that she had left and all would leave her alone. She had never stayed after sundown before, so he couldn't see why she would choose to do so tonight.

He crept over the yard, hiding in the shadows as he did. He finally made it to the edge of the riverbank, breathing through his mouth so as to not smell the Thames up so close. He crept over, listening hard as it was difficult to see in the dark.

"Hurry," he heard Fowler's voice urgently. "They'll come back, you know they will."

"On what grounds?"

"Drake, the son, he saw it all. He may not convince them to see to his own vendetta, but the Crown will certainly care about the stolen goods. But if there's nothing here when they return—"

"Then he'll look the fool."

Drake's head snapped up at the voice. He knew that voice. Had heard it far too often.

Bennett. He had been right. His pride, however, was soon tempered by how he knew Madeline would react to such news.

"Can we move it over to your factory?"

Bennett snorted. "It's not my factory yet. But it will be soon."

"Oh? I thought the woman wasn't letting you in."

"She's thinking about it," Bennett said confidently. "I've made things go poorly enough for her that she won't have much choice if she wants her father to think she has any capability remaining."

Drake had to hold back a snarl at Bennett's words.

"I'm done with waiting," Fowler said. "I'm taking care of it myself."

"What do you mean?"

"Have you ever heard of a man named Karl Maxfeld?"

Drake's blood ran cold.

"Of course," Bennett said, and Drake could hear the surprise in his voice. "He's the man Madeline married last year — or, thought she married."

"Right," Fowler said. "He was in Newgate, about to be hung. He escaped."

"So what about him?"

"He wants revenge. I want Castleton Stone, and you aren't getting the job done."

"What are you suggesting?"

It seemed Bennett finally realized he was in over his head.

"Maxfeld is going to do it for me."

"Do... what, exactly?"

Even Bennett sounded trepidatious.

"What do you think?"

Drake was already pushing himself up, scrambling to his feet and away from the bank. He wasn't going to take his chances any longer. He no longer cared about justice for his parents, no longer cared about the smuggling operation. He only cared about one thing — and that was saving the woman he loved.

The woman he loved.

For yes, he loved her. He loved her with all of his heart. That was the reason he had pushed her away, why he had tried to keep her safe. But in pushing her away from him, he'd only put her in further danger.

He had made a huge mistake. Now it might cost him Madeline. And she was everything.

He had to get to her before anyone else did.

He had to get to her now.

CHAPTER 23

"Now, now, love, that's no way to greet me."

Madeline placed a hand on her racing heart, attempting to take back control of her breath.

"What are you doing here?" she demanded, trying not to look up at the staircase in hopes that Bennett would appear once more.

"I told you I would be back if you did not give me what I asked for — what I deserve."

"You deserve what was coming for you."

"Oh, my hanging at Newgate?"

"Yes."

She inched backward, until she bumped into the table behind her. She reached a hand around her back, her fingers searching the table as surreptitiously as possible, until they closed over the instrument she had been looking for.

Madeline willed deep breaths, not wanting Maxfeld to know just how much his sudden appearance had frightened her — and how much she was still panicked.

"I have nothing to give you," she said, raising her other hand in the air. "Why will you not just leave me alone?"

"Well, here's the thing," Maxfeld said, advancing toward her, his smile sickly sweet, "you still hold the key to my financial freedom, but no longer in the way that I initially thought you would."

Madeline eyed him warily. "Just what is that supposed to mean?"

"Well, sweet, it seems that there is someone else who you have angered. Someone who is even more vindictive than I am."

"I don't understand how that has anything to do with you."

"Well, the two of us have… joined forces, you could say. He gets what he wants, and I get my revenge."

Madeline's heart beat against her ribs and she wished now that she hadn't ordered Drake to leave her, wished that she hadn't been so stubborn in her hurt. If there was ever a time she could use a little protection, it was now.

"And just how are you going to do so?"

He kept advancing toward her and she tried to step around him, but he stopped so close that she had no room to escape.

He leaned in, and she was reminded of how, at one point in time, she had welcomed his closeness, welcomed his kiss. How stupid she had been. How desperately hopeful for love, that she hadn't seen who he truly was. For now, she knew what true love was, true attraction, true passion. She had been so worried that she no longer had enough intuition to know whether or not to trust Drake, but all she had to do was compare him to Maxfeld to know that he was nothing like him, that he was, rather, the man for her. The man she could count on. The man who would always be there for her.

She turned her face to the side as she tried to push Maxfeld away with her free hand. "Get away from me."

"Come now," he said tracing a finger down the side of her

face, and she shivered in disgust. "Don't you want one last kiss?"

As he said the words, he leaned in to kiss her, and she was so busy trying to avoid his lips that she didn't realize he had raised his other hand until the fingers of both hands were at her neck holding her still — and then clenching.

She squirmed in his grip, trying to free herself, but she wasn't strong enough. His hands tightened, squeezing all breath from her, attempting to take away her life. For a moment she panicked. And then she forced herself to calm, to think — and reached around and plunged the carving knife she had been using on her sculpture into his abdomen.

His hands immediately loosened as he released her before dropping to his stomach as he gripped the small blade.

He stared at her in shock as she gasped, horrified yet free.

Maxfeld slowly started to pull the knife from his gut as he stared at her, his eyes hard with fury, and Madeline had no idea if she had inflicted any actual damage or not. But there was one thing she did know — she had to run.

She turned, but in her shock and panic, her foot got tangled in her skirts and she fell to the floor. She scrambled up, trying to make her way to the door, but suddenly a hand closed around her ankle and began pulling her backward.

"Did you really think you could run from me?" Maxfeld sneered, flipping her over and this time he brandished the knife. "I was going to be nice about this, but—"

Suddenly there was a loud pop and Maxfeld's eyes nearly bulged out of his head. He took one step backward, then another, until the knife fell from his hand and clattered to the floor.

Madeline heaved a breath, about to turn around to see just who her saviour was, when the voice she never thought she'd hear again spoke from the doorway, flooding her with every emotion imaginable — relief, thankfulness, and love.

"Madeline?" Drake called, his voice raw and gravelly. "Are you all right?"

She didn't trust herself to speak but nodded as she rolled over and turned back onto her stomach, scrambling to her feet as she sprinted toward Drake and launched herself into his arms.

He dropped his pistol as he wrapped his arms around her, holding her tighter than she could have ever imagined as he dropped kisses on her head.

"Madeline," he breathed, "thank God you are all right."

Even as he stroked her hair, Madeline could feel him looking around her, back at Maxfeld, who was still prone on the ground.

"I need to go check on him," he murmured in her ear. "Stay here. Hold the pistol."

"But—"

"Just one moment," he said, holding up a finger. "I can't risk him coming after you again."

She nodded jerkily as she picked up the pistol with distaste, holding it far away from her as she watched him walk over to Maxfeld. He leaned down, placing two fingers at his throat, before turning back to look up at her with a nod.

"He's gone," he said, his breath coming out on a sigh. "He'll never bother you again." He stopped for a second. "Madeline… what happened to him?"

"I… I stabbed him with my sculpting knife."

"Are you all right?"

Madeline could only stare at the body of the man who had caused her so much pain, so much angst, as she was flooded with relief as intense as the shock over all that had just occurred. She slowly nodded.

"I think so. I… don't know what to say." She slowly lowered the pistol beside her. "I—"

"I have something to say."

She whirled around to find another man standing at the door, a pistol in his hand as he stared at her. She raised hers in turn, although the truth was, she had no idea what she proposed to do with it. She had seen them loaded and fired before, but had never actually done any of it herself.

"Who are you?" she demanded, forcing herself to keep her voice steady.

"Why don't you introduce me, Runner?" the man asked, a glint in his steely blue eyes, and it unnerved Madeline that he actually seemed to be enjoying this entire scene in front of him.

"You aren't worthy to make her acquaintance," Drake seethed, taking slow steps toward them, his voice so full of malice that Madeline had to blink a few times.

"Very well, then," the older man said flippantly. "I am Lee Fowler," he said with a nod to Madeline, his smile sickly sweet. "You must be Miss Castleton."

"How do you know who I am?" Madeline asked, anger rising within her now. She was sick and tired of being at the mercy of men who wanted nothing from her but her money, her land, her business.

"How could I not?" he said with a shrug. "For you are—"

"Madeline!" Bennett burst through the doors behind this Fowler. "Thank goodness," he said, breathing hard when he saw her.

"Oh, bloody hell," Drake couldn't help exclaim, rolling his eyes as Bennett came near to them. "What are *you* here to do?"

"To save Madeline," Bennett said, bending over with his hands on his knees as he breathed heavily, unused to such exertions. "Fowler had locked me in a room, but I managed to escape in time."

"Would someone please tell me just what is happening

here?" Madeline asked, annoyed now and ready to shoot all of them — well, except perhaps Drake.

"Fowler is the man who killed my parents," Drake said, his voice full of such malice that it was a wonder he didn't run across the room and kill him right then and there. "He's the head of the smuggling ring my father was a part of — the very same smuggling ring that is trying to access your factory, with the help of your cousin over there."

Madeline whipped her head over to Bennett. "No," she said, shaking her head. She hadn't wanted to believe it, had convinced herself that Drake had been wrong about her cousin. "Bennett — is this true?"

"Madeline," he said, holding out a hand in supplication. "I never meant for it to come to this, you have to believe me."

"To come to what — to someone trying to kill me?" she said, her voice rising incredulously as she pointed her chin across the room to where Maxfeld lay.

"Exactly," he said with relief. "I'm so glad you understand."

"Bennett," she said, enunciating every syllable. "All that has happened with the business — has that been your doing?"

"Well… yes," he said scratching his temple. "I thought if you would let it go peacefully, tell your father to turn it over to me, that we could do all this without bloodshed, and everyone would be happy. It was what I deserved, what was supposed to happen when you married Donning — Maxfeld — and lost interest in the business. Then it all came to nothing."

"Oh, well then," she said sarcastically. "I am so sorry that my sham of a marriage and near-death was such an inconvenience to you."

"It was for all of us, Madeline," he said condescendingly and if she hadn't been holding the pistol, she would have smacked him across the face.

"Enough of this," Fowler said, his jovial attitude gone, annoyance in its place. "We're here to take the business. No one here is going to stop me as I have more men on the way. I didn't realize I would be greeted by such a party. We have a new plan."

"We do?" Bennett said, looking to him hopefully.

"We do," Fowler said. "We still kill your cousin — and her lover over there — and then the old man will have no choice but to give you the business. Hopefully he'll be so distressed it will be sooner rather than later."

"Not on my watch," Drake growled, but as he began to move toward them, Fowler lifted the pistol and pointed it, not at him but at Madeline, although he kept his eyes on Drake.

"Not another step," he said, and Madeline used the attention he held on Drake to begin inching over to the wall. "If you come any closer, I will shoot her. You might as well drop that gun, sweetheart. You have no idea how to use it."

"She might not but I most assuredly do."

Georgie, Marshall and three other Bow Street detectives stepped through the door. As soon as Georgie's voice rang out, everything happened so quickly that Madeline had trouble describing the scene afterward.

Fowler twisted around, lifted the pistol, and began to aim at Georgie as Drake went flying toward him and Madeline pulled her own trigger in the same instant.

Multiple retorts rang out through the room, until they were all standing there in eerie silence with gunpowder thick in the air around them.

Madeline breathed deeply as she saw Drake collapsed overtop of Fowler. She ran toward him, her heart beating loudly in her ears, nearly as loud as the shout of "Drake!" that rang through the room — even as she realized it came from her own mouth.

She reached him before anyone else, pushing him over to see that blood covered his chest.

"Drake, no, oh Drake, I'm so sorry, I—"

Tears flew down her face as she ran her hands over his face, his chest, his arms, too stunned to know what she should be doing to help him.

But then he sat up and cupped her face in his hands.

"Shh, Madeline, it's all right. I'm fine. You're fine. All is well."

"But—" she looked at him, before reaching in and ripping open his jacket. Beneath it his white shirt was near pristine but for a few drops of blood — and some dirt.

"It's not my blood," he said quietly. "It's his."

Madeline rocked back on her heels as she looked down at Fowler. She had shot him clean in the chest — how she had no idea — luck she supposed, but the slight rise and fall told her that he was still breathing.

"He's still alive," she said, breathing out. "Good. That's good. I know he was evil and that he killed your parents, but I would never want someone to die by my hand — even him."

"I know," Drake said as he removed his ruined jacket and threw it to the floor. "I know."

Then he reached over and wrapped his arms around her, picking her up and taking her into his lap despite all of the onlookers, and kissed her square on the lips.

They were mid-kiss when a shocked voice rang out. "Madeline?"

It was the only voice, the only thing that could cut through such a moment.

She turned quickly, her eyes flying open.

"Father?"

CHAPTER 24

"Father?"

Drake had been so lost in Madeline that he had nearly forgotten everything else around them. He most certainly had not been prepared for Ezra Castleton to step into the room.

It wasn't every day you met the father of the woman you wanted to marry.

He scrambled to his feet, aware that this was not exactly the surest way to show a man that he could protect and look after his daughter. He expected Madeline to push away from him, to put some distance between them so that she was no longer trapped in his embrace.

But she surprised him, and instead interlaced her fingers with his, then tugged on his hand to pull him across the room.

Meanwhile he noticed that Georgie, Marshall, and the two other detectives who accompanied them had crossed the room to Fowler and Bennett, and were in the process of preparing to take them to Bow Street, although if they had asked Drake, he would have told them to take them straight to Newgate. As it was, Fowler was not looking particularly healthy.

"Georgie," he said on his way by, "best get some men over to the timberyard before it's cleared out."

She nodded at him, "Already done," she said. "We should have this entire operation taken care of while you look after your lady love."

He smiled bashfully, which only caused her to laugh as he walked over to Castleton.

"Father!" Madeline stepped into the older man's embrace, and her bearded, round father with the most loving expression one could ever imagine wrapped his arms around her and held her tight.

"Oh Madeline," he said, looking around him in wonder, "what exactly have you gotten yourself into while I was gone?"

"It's a long story," she said, looking up at him with a smile, stepping back and holding her hand out to Drake once more. "But first, there is someone you should meet."

"Oh, should I?" he said, lifting his brows, and Drake stepped up with his hand extended.

"Mr. Castleton, it is a pleasure to meet you," he said. "I must tell you that I am very much in love with your daughter."

Drake wasn't sure if Castleton's bushy brows could have risen any higher, as he turned to look from Madeline to Drake and back again.

"You're the Bow Street Runner."

It was likely the first time Drake had ever kept himself from correcting the reference as he didn't think it was the best way to win Castleton over.

"Yes, that's right."

"You helped save Madeline last year."

"Well," Drake cringed, "I tried. But Maxfeld escaped."

He motioned across the room.

"And now?"

"Now he will never hurt your daughter again. No one will. I promise you."

He had been so intent on his conversation with Castleton that he hadn't noticed Madeline staring at him in wonder.

"Are you all right?" he asked her, hoping that she hadn't been injured any more than he had thought.

"I am," she said, her voice just above a whisper. "Did you just say... that you love me?"

"I did," he said with a quick nod, noting that Georgie winked at him as she passed.

"I'll, ah... I'll give you two a moment," Castleton said, clearing his throat. "It seems I need to go have a word with my nephew."

Drake no longer cared about anything else that was happening around them as he took Madeline's hands within his.

"Madeline," he said reverently, noting that her bare hands were covered in clay, and he absentmindedly rubbed some of it off, "I was a fool."

"You were."

"I said things to you that are unforgiveable, I realize that. I know it sounds flippant to tell you that I didn't mean any of it, and I am aware that an apology can never be enough. But you have to know that I said them to push you away. I thought... I thought that if you were with me, you would be in too much danger. My mother was killed because of my father's actions. But by pushing you away, the only result was that I wasn't there to protect you when you needed me the most. And for that I am so sorry. I don't know if you can ever forgive me, but I need you to know just how much I love you."

She looked down for a moment, and when she finally

returned his gaze, her eyes were glistening with unshed tears.

"Oh, Drake," she said, then paused, tilting her head to the side. "I wasn't good to you either. I was so afraid to trust again. To trust in you, yes, but most importantly, to trust in myself. I was so concerned with the past that I didn't focus on the future, and the present. On what you were showing me, on the man you were." Her voice softened. "I know you didn't mean those things. I realized belatedly what you were trying to do. And even when I tried to push you from my mind, it seems that you wouldn't leave."

She laughed lowly as she led him over to the artist's corner of the factory. She turned a sculpture on the table around so that he could see it.

And looked into a reflection.

"I came to sculpt, to think, to allow my mind to wander. But all I could think about was you."

"Madeline," he breathed, "this is… unbelievable. Not so much the subject, but your talent."

"She's something, isn't she?" Ezra Castleton approached them once more, placing a hand on his daughter's shoulder. "What is this?"

"It's a new stone," she said, obviously hesitant at first, but then Drake was proud when Madeline lifted her chin confidently.

"I see," he said, lifting a brow. "Well, it seems much has happened in my time away — here, and in Bath. I know its late, but what do you say we have dinner?"

"I think that sounds like a fine idea," Madeline said as Castleton turned away. As Madeline went to follow him, however, Drake raised his hand.

"Goodbye, Madeline."

"Goodbye?" She turned around to face him. "Just where do you think you are going?"

"Well, I... " his voice broke and he cleared his throat, "I know you forgive me and everything, but I figured that after all that happened, we would go our separate ways."

"Is that what you want?" she asked defiantly, fighting her inclination to lower her head and instead lifting her chin, challenging him.

"No," he shook his head, unable to hold back his emotion any longer. He didn't care if she knew how he felt — in fact, he needed her to. "I want you, Madeline. I want you in my life. In fact, I need you in it. If you will have me."

She sucked in a breath, her eyes once again glistening but she said nothing as his own tears welled, and he blinked them away as rapidly as he could. He didn't cry. He never cried. He hadn't felt the sensation of tears since the day he found out his parents were gone.

He would not cry now.

Or maybe he would.

As Madeline reached up and wiped the tear away, he took a shaky breath.

"Madeline," he said, cupping her face in his hands, "you are the woman I never knew I needed. I know that I may not be the man you ever thought you would end up with but I love you to the point it hurts. You've broken down all of the walls I had built up around myself — torn them down with such ferocity. If you don't want me, I understand, truly I do. But I need to know now, before I lose my heart to you any further."

"Drake," she whispered, "you haven't lost your heart."

"Oh, but I have."

"No," she shook her head. "You've lost nothing. You've only gained a heart — mine. We share ours now with one another. I love you, too. More than I can possibly explain with words. You believe in me. You see strength within me that I didn't even know I had. I may not be like Georgie, or like Alice, and I doubted myself for so long, but you helped prove to me that I can look out for myself, that I can have you support me and still stand on my own feet. The thought of not having you in my life, however… that is more than I can bear."

"Oh, Madeline," he said, tilting his head and resting his forehead upon hers. "You are the most amazing woman I have ever met and I am so blessed to know you. Will you…" He swallowed hard, "will you be my wife?"

"Absolutely," she said, her lips curling before she leaned in and kissed him with such promise that it took his breath away.

When they finally broke apart, he took her hand in his. "It seems your father and I have something to discuss tonight."

"That you do," she said with a laugh. "That you do."

CHAPTER 25

Madeline had trouble letting Drake go even for the short hour until dinner at her father's house.

Despite the fact that Drake had just spoken the most wonderful words she had ever heard in her entire life — those asking her to be his wife — she was still concerned about the outcome of all that had occurred tonight.

What if Fowler did die from the wounds she had inflicted upon him? He was a most despicable human being, of course, but the thought of actually killing another person by her own hand... it was more than she could bear.

"Is everything all right, Sweetling?"

She looked up, forcing a smile at her father's use of the nickname from her childhood.

"Hopefully it will be," she said with a sigh. "I'm sorry I didn't write to you earlier."

She'd told him, briefly, all that had occurred while he had been gone — the smuggling ring, Bennett's involvement and his attempts to control the business, and how she had asked Drake for help.

Ezra had been shocked, but he had held in his thoughts about it all until she had finished speaking.

He stroked his beard now as he eyed her.

"You know, Madeline, I'm not sure I know a man who would entrust his business to his daughter."

"I know, Father."

"I do not trust you with the business *because* you are my daughter."

"You don't?" She looked up at that.

"No," he shook his head. "I entrust the business with you because you are the most capable person I have ever met in my life. Sure, I may have a bit of a bias, but I also know you better than I know anyone else. And if the past year has proven anything, it is that you are capable of taking whatever life throws at you and overcoming it. No, I do not like to hear that you had to face such adversity once more, especially in my absence. That most certainly was never my intention. But… at the same time, I am proud of you for how you handled it. You understood who you could trust."

"I thought I could trust Bennett," she said bitterly.

"Well, so did I," Ezra said.

"Why did you ask him to watch over me? You didn't… quite think I could do it? I understand but—"

"I never asked him that," Ezra said, shaking his head. "I asked him to help you. I see now that was wrong. But you never did trust him — not completely."

"No," she said, tilting her head in consideration, "not completely."

"You see?" her father said, lifting a hand toward her, "Your intuition isn't that far off, after all."

She slightly smiled for him. "I guess you are right. Now, tell me, how was Bath?"

"Wonderful," he said, his smile widening farther than she thought she had ever seen it before. "I have much to share."

The carriage came to a stop just then, and Madeline began to ask him more, but he shook his head. "I am not going to share it with you alone, however." He tucked her hand into the crook of his elbow. "Let's go inside and get you freshened up. Then I'll share all once Drake arrives for supper. We are to have a few other guests as well."

"Oh?" she asked, eyeing him mischievously. "Would one of those guests happen to be Lady Susan?"

He threw back his head and laughed, long and loud. How she had missed that laugh.

"Yes, she will be in attendance. As will Alice and her husband, and a friend who is in London."

"Oh, that must be Rose," Madeline said. "Would you mind overly if I invited one more?"

He shook his head. "The more the merrier," he said, "but you had better hurry as the dinner hour will be upon us soon."

She nodded and rushed off to write a note to Georgie before she did as her father suggested and changed. Her father was back, and her friends and the man who loved her would be joining them soon.

The worst night of her life had turned into one of the best.

* * *

DRAKE WAS surprised when Georgie received a message to join the late dinner at the Castleton household. She told him she didn't have to come, but if Madeline had asked for her presence, then she must want her there.

The two of them finished their business at Bow Street as quickly as possible before making their way there.

"Well, Drake," Georgie asked as they approached the red brick townhouse, "what's it like?"

"What's what like?"

"Finishing work and having someone to go home to?" she raised an eyebrow at him.

"I suppose I never really thought of it like that," he said as they knocked on the door, "but I think I rather like the idea."

She smiled at him before the door opened and they stepped through to the foyer, and Drake was shocked to find that a chorus of voices from a room beyond greeted them. They entered to find that in addition to Madeline and her father, an elderly woman who must be her aunt accompanied them, as well as Benjamin and Alice Luxington, Lady Susan, and Rose Ellis.

"Good evening," he said, nodding to them all, and they responded in turn.

"What happened?" Madeline asked, standing to greet as they entered.

Drake sighed as he took her arm and settled himself into the chesterfield next to her, enjoying her touch and the knowledge that he had a partner who would always be there at the end of the day — no matter how badly it had gone.

"Well, Maxfeld is dead," he said, as the entire room focused their attention on him. "He will never bother you again," he said, looking at Madeline, taking her hand within his, uncaring what anyone might think by his show of affection. "Fowler is alive still, but with all of his crimes — as well as those who are willing to speak against him — he will hang in Newgate, sooner rather than later."

Madeline nodded and squeezed his hand.

"I must say I am glad that I wasn't the one to kill him," she said quietly. "I know he murdered your parents, Drake, and I hate him for that, but I'm not sure if I could have lived with myself if I had."

He returned the pressure of her fingers and nodded. "I know. And I'm glad that it wasn't at your hand either, although I will always be grateful that you saved me." He paused. "As for your cousin… " he looked from Madeline to her father with a shrug, "that is somewhat up to you. We can throw him in the stocks if you'd like."

"No," Ezra Castleton said grimly. "I'll handle Bennett."

"What are you going to do?" Madeline asked her father, looking up at him with curiosity and Ezra smirked.

"I am going to show him exactly what happens when you go against your family — against those who have trusted you and looked after you your entire life. I am going to show him what it means to be alone, without money. He will have to look after himself from now on. And if he ever — and I mean *ever* — comes near Castleton Stone again, I will have him thrown out on his arse."

"Where I will pick him up and take him off to prison," Drake said with a nod.

"Well, this has all been quite thrilling," Alice said from her place on the sofa across the room. "Adventure follows you wherever you go, Madeline!"

Madeline laughed lightly. "And I am sure your next question will be just when you can begin writing about it."

"Madeline!" Alice exclaimed before she laughed. "All right, yes. But only if you don't mind. And when you are ready."

"We'll talk about that," Madeline said, rolling her eyes.

It wasn't long before they filed into the dining room, and no sooner had they taken their seats than Alice and Madeline were eying their parents with a look of much interest.

"So," Madeline said, taking a sip of the well-earned drink in front of her, "are the two of you going to tell us anything about Bath?"

Lady Susan blushed as pink as a young debutante at her first ball, and Ezra choked slightly on his whiskey.

"There's not much to tell," Lady Susan said primly,

although a smile played on her lips, "although it was most interesting that we both happened to be visiting at the same time."

"Oh, so *very* interesting," Alice said sarcastically, and then she and Madeline began laughing.

Ezra sighed dramatically before his lips began to curve up at the edges.

"Oh, very well," he said. "Lady Susan and I… are going to be married."

Madeline and Alice exchanged a look before they began talking at the same time, as a cheer resounded around the table.

"It's a night for celebration!" Alice said, raising her glass, and soon they all began to do the same.

Drake sat back in his chair and stared round at all of them, awed that he was so suddenly part of this — of a family, a group of friends who cared for one another, who were excited about moments in one another's lives.

He supposed that was what it meant to love someone.

After the dishes had finally be cleared away and the party stood to retire to the drawing room, Drake approached Castleton.

"Ah, Mr. Castleton," he said, shocked at the nerves that began flying around his stomach. He was a grown man, one who had faced down bullets and the nastiest of criminals that London had to offer. Why was he nervous about speaking with a stone maker? "Do you think we could have a moment to ourselves?"

"Of course, Son," Castleton said, placing a meaty hand on Drake's shoulder, and for a moment he was returned to his uncle. His stomach began to sink as he thought of their last conversation.

What must his uncle be thinking right now? Drake had

been so terrible to him, and all Andrew had been trying to do was protect him. Drake's first order of business would be to pay them a visit — but first, time for one of the most important conversations he would ever have.

CHAPTER 26

Madeline stared up at the wooden house which was clearly in need of repairs. The fact that Drake had invited her here meant more than she could have explained to him. He had always been so closed off about his past that to show her this building, to introduce her to his aunt and uncle… it seemed to be his way of sharing with her who he was, where his life began, and how he became the man he was today.

"Are you ready?" she asked him. It was mid-afternoon the day following the final showdown at the factory and the night of revelations at her father's house. When Drake had told her about his plans to visit his aunt and uncle, she had asked if she could come along and had been pleasantly surprised when he had agreed.

She could only hope her meeting with them would go as well as that of her father and Drake apparently had last night.

When she had asked Drake what had been said, he had only pulled her in tight, placed a kiss on her forehead, and promised her that he would always take care of her.

She had returned in kind, and he had burst into laughter.

"Do you always knock?" she asked when he did, and he shrugged.

"Yes," he said, seemingly surprised at her question. "They always tell me not to, but somehow I never felt it was my place to just... enter."

"Of course it is your place," she said lifting an eyebrow. "You are like a son to them. It's what they would want."

He nodded and placed his hand on the doorknob, turning and opening the door, surprising his uncle, who was just walking toward it down the hall.

"Drake," he said, his brows lifting, and Madeline was surprised by how much Drake looked like his uncle. It wasn't so much their physical features, but more so, the way he carried himself as he waved them in. "And who is this lovely woman?"

"This is Madeline," he said, reaching an arm around her and tucking her into his side. "She... she's going to be my wife. Madeline, this is my Uncle Andrew and my Aunt—"

Before he could continue, there was a shriek from the kitchen, and a woman who must be his aunt came running around the corner. "Your wife! Oh, Drake."

The woman Madeline knew must be his Aunt Mabel pulled first Drake into an embrace and then Madeline, who returned it warmly while Drake looked on with wide eyes. It seemed that stifling one's emotions was typically an entire family trait. Except for today.

His aunt was already wiping her eyes as she pulled them into the sitting room.

Before they could ask any further questions about Madeline or how their relationship had come to be, Drake took a breath and looked his uncle square in the eye.

"Uncle Andrew," he said, "I've also come to apologize for yesterday. For the things I said, for how I treated you. I was angry and looking for someone to blame everything on. It shouldn't have been you. You've done nothing but provide a home for me, protect me, and support me in every way possible. I'm sorry."

His uncle was silent for a moment, simply regarding Drake, before reaching out slowly and placing a hand on Drake's knee.

"You have nothing to be sorry for, Son," he said, his voice low and rough. "I understand what you meant and I'm sorry you had to find out the way you did. I would have been angry, too. I *have* been angry about your parents' death for so long now. I just… I always promised that I would watch out for you. That *we* would watch out for you. We never wanted to see you hurt."

"And I thank you for that," Drake said, releasing a breath. "It's done now. It's over."

"What happened?" his uncle said, and then Drake sat back and explained all.

Madeline watched him speak, her heart melting when she saw the emotions he allowed to cross his face, how he got choked up when he told of her part in the scene, how he actually admitted how scared he had been and how, finally, it had all worked out in the end.

He let out a breath when he finished, and his uncle only blinked at him. "My God," he breathed. "It's done, then."

"It's done." Drake nodded. "I understand why you didn't want me involved, but I must say, to know that it's over, that justice has been served to those who murdered my parents… it does bring a sense of closure."

"That it does," his uncle said with a heavy sigh. "That it does."

After his aunt insisted on feeding them, Drake and Madeline left the house hand-in-hand, with a promise to visit again soon — and to be married in only a few weeks.

"Are you sure?" Drake asked, stopping in the street and

tilting Madeline's face up to look at him. "Are you still sure you want to be married to me?"

"I have never been more sure of anything in my entire life," Madeline said, a smile spreading across her face. "Now," she said, "I have a suggestion."

"Let's hear it."

"You live close to here."

"I do."

"If I will be living there soon, then I think I had better come see what can be done with your place. There is much to do to prepare it."

Drake laughed dryly. "There is no denying that."

"And..." she leaned in to his ear and whispered, "perhaps we best start with the bedroom."

He grinned. "A fine idea."

He took her hand and practically ran with her down the road until they made it to his home, and he pulled her up the stairs, until they reached the top floor when he bent down and picked her up.

"Drake!" she exclaimed.

He grinned at her impishly, nearly taking her aback. For Drake hardly ever grinned, let alone... *impishly*.

"Who *are* you?" she said in wonder, and he winked at her.

"I am a man in love. A man who is, finally, allowing himself to love. A man who is going to show you just how much he loves you, in the best way he knows how."

And with that, he laid her gently on the bed, as though she was a porcelain statue.

"I'm not that fragile," she said with a laugh, and he pounced onto the bed beside her.

"I know," he said with a nod.

"I promise you," she said, curling a hand around his neck, "that I will not break. That I will be here for you. That I can also do an excellent job looking after myself."

"I know," he repeated, smiling wickedly. "But there are certain things that I can do much better."

She looked at him in consternation for a moment before he began to inch down her body, and her lips rounded in an 'O' when she realized just exactly what he meant.

He didn't waste time undressing her, but instead lifted her skirts and began to slide his hands up her legs, each touch sending a thrill through her, her skin tingling as he traveled up, higher and higher, until he finally reached the very center of her, where she was, apparently, waiting for him.

"Madeline," he said, his voice somewhat sing-song, and when he ran his fingers over her abdomen, she giggled, pushing them away.

"Stop!" she cried out through her laughter, and he moved back an inch.

"Stop? You're sure?" he said, his voice somewhat crestfallen but understanding.

"Oh no!" she said, reaching down to pull him back. "Not stop — not there. Certainly not. No, I only meant, well, I'm a bit ticklish."

"Ah," he said, his voice muffled from beneath her skirts, "I shall remember that."

"You mean to use it against me, don't you?" she said, with a sigh, as suddenly his touch was no longer ticklish whatsoever.

"I just might," he said. "But for now—"

And then his mouth was on her and she gasped in shock, all laughter gone as he did things that she could only describe as delightfully sinful, and yet, oh, so *right*.

He swirled his tongue around the very core of her pleasure as his fingers found her, one, then two, in and out until she was moving against him of her own accord, her head thrown back and her hands fisted in the sheet.

She had never known anything like this, and wondered if she ever would again. This didn't seem like anything that could ever be replicated, so wonderful did it feel, and then... and then—

She couldn't breathe, so caught off guard was she by the release of explosion around her, and she cried out Drake's name in a voice so loud, so strong, that she almost didn't even realize it was her own.

When she finally came back down, it was to find that Drake had extricated himself from her skirts and was now posing on top of them, his chin on his folded hands above her knee as he watched her.

"That..." he said, raising his brows, "was incredible."

She managed a short laugh. "Is that not what I am supposed to say?"

"Perhaps," he said with a shrug, "but I can only be honest and tell you that I enjoyed it just as much as you did... if not more."

Finally regaining all of her senses, she lifted herself up from the bed, and he sat up, waiting for her. She reached out, grabbed his hands, and surprised him by pulling him forward, clumsily, until he finally realized her goal and lay back before her.

"Now," she said, her hands coming to the fall of his trousers, "it's your turn."

"Madeline," he said, lifting a hand to her hair, which she realized was bouncing around her shoulders now, "you don't have to do that,"

"I know," she said, "but I want to. Only—"

"Yes?"

"Will you tell me if I'm doing it right?"

"I don't see how you could do it any other way."

She waited a moment, and he finally nodded.

"Of course."

She worked to spring him free, waving off any attempts to help he provided, before she lightly ran a hand over him. He groaned, and she smiled in response, for it meant that she was doing something right. He slid a hand over hers, moving it up and down, showing her just exactly what felt good, and she soon had the rhythm herself, only to lean down and place her mouth upon the very tip of him.

"Madeline," he said, his voice a pant, and she smiled over him, at the power that surged through her in knowing that she had such a man at her mercy.

She slid her lips over him, taking him fully into her mouth, before moving up and down, her hand below sliding over what she couldn't take in. His fingers twined into her hair, but he didn't push her or move her as he allowed her to set the pace — a pace which he must have enjoyed, for his breath came quicker and he groaned her name aloud.

"Madeline," he said. "I want *you* — all of you."

"I would love that," she said so enthusiastically that he managed a choked laugh before flipping her over, lifting her skirts, and then, in one swift motion, burying himself deep inside her.

She felt full, complete, and wanted nothing more than for him to go deeper, faster, harder, with every thrust. In no time at all, he was staring deeply into her eyes, biting his lip before he cried out her name and spent himself inside her.

She held onto him as he came, until finally he collapsed next to her, although he threw out an arm and caught her close beside him as he placed a kiss on her temple.

"Oh, Madeline," he said. "You... you make me feel... everything. You just make me *feel*." He ran a hand through his hair. "I haven't allowed that for myself in a very long time."

"Well, then, I'm glad that you have now," she said, sliding a hand over his cheek.

"It's frightening," he admitted, his lids hiding his eyes for a moment. "I still worry that something could happen to you. I have no idea how I would ever survive it."

She pushed herself up so that she was leaning on one elbow, staring down at him.

"I understand better than most," she said. "But when you try to escape the sadness of life, then you escape all of your good emotions — the joy, the love that makes life worth living. I learned that the hard way."

She paused for a moment. "I never thought I would love again. I didn't trust myself, wasn't sure that I could ever find a man who wouldn't hurt me. But in you… I did."

She smiled at him then, loving the man he had been, the man he was, and the man he would become.

He reached out and drew her close to him once more.

"I love you, Madeline."

"And I love you, Drake."

EPILOGUE

Madeline knew he was there before he even said anything.

"Good afternoon," she said, smiling down at the sculpture in front of her. "And why am I so lucky to have a visit from London's finest detective?"

She placed the tool down in front of her before looking up with a smile at her husband, so dapper in his black trousers and jacket.

Hands in his pockets, he strolled toward her, nodding his greeting to the sculptors nearby.

"Must a man need an excuse to gaze upon his wife?"

She folded her arms across her chest.

"He does when he is currently assigned to one of London's most prominent murder investigations."

He laughed, turning a few heads of other men, who likely thought him somewhat ridiculous to be laughing when they were discussing such a subject.

But that was the way it was — one had to put the work aside to enjoy time with his loved ones, or else he would drive himself mad.

He had learned that the hard way.

"As it happens…" he said, "I must visit one of London's finest inns. I am likely to get much further if I appear to be entering with a woman." He leaned in beside her ear, "A high-class paramour, perhaps?"

She raised a brow.

"Just what are you suggesting?"

"That you might want to do some undercover detecting with me?" he asked with a raised brow. "Nothing dangerous today. Just to survey the hotel and find some information."

"Well," she said, pulling out her pocket watch, shocked to find that the afternoon was nearly gone, "as it happens, I have just completed this fine-looking gargoyle in front of me, forged out of the new Castleton Stone. And I know the company owner."

She said it quietly enough that no one else could hear, but she smiled at him mischievously, and he raised her hand to his lips as he helped her out around the table.

"Are you happy with your decision?" he asked as he led her out of the factory.

"I am," she said decidedly. "Clark has helped manage this company for the past few years. Together, he and I will do a fine job running the business, especially as my father will stay on to advise us for a time. It's hard to believe that he has actually decided to take a step back. I know he always said he would, but I never thought it would come to pass."

"Well, marriage can do strange things to a man," Drake said with a low chuckle as he opened the door for her, and they both gazed out at the sun setting over the Thames.

"That it can," she said, looking over at him. "That it can."

Drake himself was proof of that. He was still Drake, the same man she had met, who had found his way into her heart, and yet he was also more than that. He now showed her a side of himself that she hadn't known was there — a vulnerable side, one that had no qualms in presenting to her just how much he loved her, that would do anything for her — anything she asked, and more.

Such as allowing her into his life as a detective. When she had told him she didn't want to be shut off from his work, wanted to know his day, wanted to feel his frustrations and be there to physically help when she could, he had been wary but had trusted her — and had found that she was of more assistance than he could have ever expected.

They were nearly at the hotel when Madeline spied a familiar figure in the distance.

"Does that look like Rose to you?" she asked, looking up at Drake, who craned his neck and nodded.

"It does."

She was standing near the entrance of the hotel, pacing back and forth, and Madeline nearly ran to catch her, so frantic was her expression.

"Rose!" she called, and Rose turned to look at her. "Is everything all right?" Madeline asked breathlessly.

"No," she said, shaking her head back and forth, her bonnet flying askew around her. "Nothing is all right." She looked past Madeline. "I have to go."

"But, Rose—"

"I must," she said, and was about to push away when Drake reached out and passed a card toward her.

"Come see me," he said firmly. "We can help."

Rose palmed the card, nodded, and then took off into a run, leaving Drake and Madeline staring at one another incredulously.

"I hope she's all right," Madeline said.

"And I hope that we are able to help her."

"You can help anyone," Madeline said, squeezing his arm underneath her hand. "Of that, I am sure. There will be no child in London better looked after than ours."

Drake's head snapped around to her so quickly that Madeline thought he must have injured his neck.

"Do you mean, future children... that we might have?"

"Yes," she said thoughtfully. "But there is one in particular that I am thinking of."

She glanced down at her stomach, and Drake's eyes nearly bulged out of his head.

"Are you sure?"

"Absolutely," she said with a grin of her own, and Drake let out a celebratory shout before picking her up and swinging her around. She laughed before looking around them.

"Are we not supposed to be undercover?"

"Is there anything more undercover than a man in love?" he asked, and she smiled. "I suppose not."

And with that, he kissed her, right in the middle of London's College Street, unafraid to show the world just how much he loved her.

THE END

AUTHOR'S NOTE

I so hope you enjoyed Madeline and Drake's story.

As with most of the books from The Bluestocking Scandals series, our heroine is very loosely based on a historical figure from the Regency era.

Eleanor Coade ran her business which created statues, architectural decorations, and garden ornaments out of Coade Stone for fifty years — from 1769 until her death in 1821. She had one of the most successful businesses of the time in an industry that was dominated by men. She bought the business herself after successfully running a linen drapery for a few years prior. Coade Stone was one of the most popular building materials of its time. The ceramic material, the recipe of which was a closely guarded secret, was quite resistant to weathering and erosion. From the Lambeth factory, her sculptures and architectural elements were sent throughout England.

Her life was quite intriguing and if you are interested in learning more, there are numerous biographies describing the life of this extraordinary woman.

AUTHOR'S NOTE

***

I would love to stay in touch with you! Sign-up for my newsletter and "Unmasking a Duke," a regency romance novella, will come straight to your inbox!

www.elliestclair.com/ellies-newsletter

You will also receive links to giveaways, sales, updates, launch information, promos, and the newest recommended reads. I hope you will join us!

A NOBLE EXCAVATION

Preview Rose's story, book 7 of The Bluestocking Scandals…

AN EXCERPT

It was good to be back.

But also slightly heartbreaking as well.

Rose's brother had welcomed her with both pity and despair – his sympathy for her obviously at odds with his own worry for how their small business would fare in the wake of the claims of fraud. Rose understood. He used the earnings from the shop to support himself and their mother, and she couldn't help but feel chagrin that she had let down the people who needed her the most.

And all for what? To further her own ego? For her desperate wish to be accepted as a scientist on equal footing of true scientists?

She was only where she was on account of a bit of luck and wealthy men's interest in her discoveries. That was all.

Rose stood now on the rise of the cliff, looking out over the shore that stretched in front of her.

She had been gone a couple of months now, which was ample time for landslides to have uncovered new stretches of rock, where fossils might be hiding.

She whistled to Digger, who was himself excitedly

searching, and he came running toward her but stopped, his attention captured by something in the distance.

"What is it?" she asked, shading her eyes with her hand, but she couldn't make out anything unusual, although a slight smattering of fog still covered the air in front of her. "Is there some animal out there?"

Digger barked in return, although Rose couldn't be sure if he was answering her or calling out to something – or some*one* in the distance.

Suddenly she started in surprise as a hulking mass rose out through the fog, bounding toward them in – joy, she realized.

Digger jumped up in answer, and soon the two dogs were circling one another with the excited interest of two new canine acquaintances.

"Hello, there," Rose said, bending to greet the dog, although she didn't have to bend far. She wasn't overly tall, and she imagined if the dog jumped up, she could plant her paws on her shoulders and they would be able to look each other straight in the eye. "Wherever did you come from?"

She had never seen the animal before, and she was fairly familiar with all who lived in the area – human or pet.

The dog barked up at her, her ears lifting as he looked backward, as though she was telling Rose that she was not alone.

She had no worry about being watched, however – anyone who would choose a dog such as this for a companion would have to be a lovely presence indeed.

"Care to join us for a walk?" she asked, and the dog barked again. She laughed. "Well, come on then."

Digger and his new friend began to excitedly play as they followed her, wrestling with one another before zipping around in circles in front of, behind, and around her. Peace settled over Rose as she allowed herself to enjoy the moment, forgetting all that had recently occupied every moment of her thoughts and her time.

Letting the dogs play, she returned her attention to the ground before her, keeping her eyes sharp for any sign of a disturbance or protrusion. It was here she had found her first skeletons, and here where she knew there must be more.

Although she was worried. Had she been gone too long? Had she left her beach exposed for any other fortune hunter to search themselves?

She was halfway down the beach when the hairs on her arms began to stand on end and she became very aware that she was being watched. She couldn't have said how she knew, but she was being drawn over toward the copse of trees in the distance, that stood sentry over their cliff and all of the shore and ocean beyond it.

"Hello?" she called out, knowing she should be concerned at the thought of being happened upon alone, but she was more so annoyed that whoever was above her had instead chosen to watch her from the distance in anonymity. "Who's there?"

Finally a bit of motion from her right had her head swiveling – and then the figure caught the attention of the dogs, who went practically galloping toward him.

Him. That much she could make out from her current position. He wore a top hat low over his eyes, and he was holding something in his hands, something he was suddenly quite intent upon. Was he trying to avoid her? The fog had lifted, and the sun was beginning to beat down upon her rather intensely, so much so that she had to lift a hand to her eyes to shield them.

"Digger!" she called out, hoping the dog would come back quickly.

She was to be disappointed, for Digger was so focused on

his new friend that he didn't seem to have any inclination to return to her.

She sighed and began trudging up the hill, onto the black charcoal of the cliffs and away from the sandy beach. Around the small circle of trees were cliffs rising high on either side, and it was almost like descending into the darkness, into the shadows and away from the light as she went.

As Rose neared, she realized that the object was a sketchpad. She looked back over her shoulder at the landscape beyond her, seeing why this would be a seat of choice for any artist.

"Good afternoon," she said as she approached, wondering if the man was ever going to look up. "I'm sorry to disturb you, I—"

"Stop."

He held out a hand and Rose did as he said, so shocked was she by the sudden directive.

"I'm sorry?"

"Stop right there," he said, still holding out his left hand as his right flew across the page in front of him. "That's perfect."

She looked around her, finding nothing in particular to note.

"What's perfect?"

"You."

Rose opened her mouth but then had to close it again, for she was at a loss for words.

"Me?"

"Yes," he said. "The light is perfect. Your stance is perfect. Your face – yes, that's it – don't move it."

Rose could only widen her eyes as her lips remained parted while she stared at this fascinating man. Who was he?

"Are you sketching me?" she couldn't help but ask as the dogs began to run circles, from her to him and back again.

"I am."

"Why?"

Finally, he lifted his head, but when he did, she rather wished he hadn't.

For he was one of the most handsome men she had ever seen. Strands of light hair peeked out from beneath his hat, while his eyes were the color of the sea behind her, a blue-green aqua that she wasn't sure could ever have been accurately captured within anything outside of nature.

She had been wrong.

"Wh-who..." she stammered, but then swallowed her nerves, berating herself for acting the fool. "Who are you?"

He tilted his head to the side as he considered her through slightly narrowed eyes.

"Perry."

"Perry?" she asked. "That's it?"

He smiled, his face warming considerably when he did so – a warmth that traveled from his lips down through her to a place she couldn't accurately describe. She had no idea why Perry didn't want to reveal his actual identity to her. She could tell from his speech that he was well-educated, if not gently bred. He couldn't be from anywhere around here.

"And who are you?" he asked in return, leaning one forearm against his bent knee in a most casual position.

"Rose," she said, not providing him with anything more than he had given her.

"Rose," he repeated, her name sounding rather sensual upon his lips. "And what brings you to Lyme Regis, Rose?"

A hot trickle of awareness began to creep down her spine, and Rose looked around for Digger to see if he was ready to resume their walk, but it seemed her faithful companion had abandoned her for another.

"I live here," she answered simply.

"Do you?" he raised his brows. "Why have I never seen you here before?"

"Do *you* live here, sir?"

"From time to time."

"Then I suppose our paths simply have not had reason to cross in the past," she said.

She couldn't help it. This man intrigued her.

"Can I see it?" she asked, gesturing to his sketchpad. His smile fell somewhat.

"Not yet."

"Why not?"

"It's just a rough sketch. I haven't finished."

"Don't tell me you are shy," she teased, surprised when he flinched slightly.

"I usually am, as it happens."

He looked down for a moment, and Rose's heart went out to this man whose cheeks flushed bright red from a few exchanged bits of conversation with her. He was handsome, yes, she had been right about that, but he was also… bashful. Endearing. She was curious to learn more.

"Very well," she said. "You may sketch me, but I will not stand here like a fool. I shall sit over here, far enough away that I cannot see what you are doing."

She folded her skirts beneath her and sat down upon a large rock that she had assumed at one point of time had been part of the cliffs above.

He looked up at her, and suddenly his slight awkwardness vanished as he flipped over the piece of paper on his sketchpad and began drawing anew.

His features lit up as became engrossed in his work, and Rose had the feeling that it was only with a piece of charcoal in his hands that he was truly comfortable.

"Are you drawing me again?"

"I am."

"You must be lacking people to pose for you, then?"

He grunted his negative response as he shook his head.

"I'm lacking people like you."

"Meaning?"

"Beautiful yet striking. Different yet captivating."

Rose's cheeks warmed at his words. She had the sense he had not said them as a compliment, but rather as his truth, which somehow made them all the more sincere.

She bit her lip as she looked down, her eyelids fluttering down as she was unsure just how to respond.

"I—thank you," she decided on simply and he nodded.

"Your dog is lovely," she said, to which he chuckled lowly, a sound that vibrated through her.

"I'm not sure if lovely is the proper term to describe Onyx," he said.

"Onyx?"

He nodded. "For her color. It's not very original, I suppose."

"Only an artist would choose such an elaborate name for a color. Digger seems quite taken with her."

She gestured out toward the beach, where the dogs were still playing in the sand.

"Digger?"

"So named for our favorite pastime."

"Your favorite pastime as well?" He looked up at her, confusion etched on his face.

"Yes," she said, "that's what we do here on the beach – we dig."

"For what?"

She opened her mouth to reply, but before she could do so, a long, low rumble resounded around them. Perry twisted his head from one side to the other, looking to see where it had come from, but Rose didn't have to – she was all too well aware that the only place to look was up.

As she did, a streak of fear laced through her. For the rock that was vibrating, the rock about to slide down the cliff – was right above Perry.

* * *

A Noble Excavation is available through Amazon and Kindle Unlimited.

Join my newsletter for updates (and you will also receive a free book!): http://elliestclair.com/ellies-newsletter.

ALSO BY ELLIE ST. CLAIR

The Bluestocking Scandals
Designs on a Duke
Inventing the Viscount
Discovering the Baron
The Valet Experiment
Writing the Rake
Risking the Detective
A Noble Excavation

The Victorian Highlanders
Callum's Vow
Finlay's Duty
Adam's Call
Roderick's Purpose
Peggy's Love

Blooming Brides
A Duke for Daisy
A Marquess for Marigold
An Earl for Iris
A Viscount for Violet

The Blooming Brides Box Set: Books 1-4

The Unconventional Ladies
Lady of Mystery

Lady of Fortune
Lady of Providence
Lady of Charade

Happily Ever After
The Duke She Wished For
Someday Her Duke Will Come
Once Upon a Duke's Dream
He's a Duke, But I Love Him
Loved by the Viscount
Because the Earl Loved Me

Happily Ever After Box Set Books 1-3
Happily Ever After Box Set Books 4-6

Searching Hearts
Duke of Christmas (prequel)
Quest of Honor
Clue of Affection
Hearts of Trust
Hope of Romance
Promise of Redemption

Searching Hearts Box Set (Books 1-5)

Standalone
Unmasking a Duke
The Stormswept Stowaway
Christmastide with His Countess
Her Christmas Wish
Merry Misrule

House of Devon

A Touch of Temptation

ABOUT THE AUTHOR

Ellie has always loved reading, writing, and history. For many years she has written short stories, non-fiction, and has worked on her true love and passion -- romance novels.

In every era there is the chance for romance, and Ellie enjoys exploring many different time periods, cultures, and geographic locations. No matter when or where, love can always prevail. She has a particular soft spot for the bad boys of history, and loves a strong heroine in her stories.

Ellie and her husband love nothing more than spending time at home with their two sons and Husky cross. Ellie can typically be found at the lake in the summer, pushing the stroller all year round, and, of course, with her computer in her lap or a book in hand.

She also loves corresponding with readers, so be sure to contact her!

www.elliestclair.com
ellie@elliestclair.com

Printed in Great Britain
by Amazon